U0025501

Little Women

小婦人

Original Author	Louisa May Alcott
Adaptor	Winnie Huang
Proofreaders	Dennis Le Boeuf / Liming Jing
Illustrator	Nan Jun

WORDS
1000

MP3

Let's Enjoy Masterpieces!

All the beautiful fairy tales and masterpieces that you have encountered during your childhood remain as warm memories in your adulthood. This time, let's indulge in the world of masterpieces through English. You can enjoy the depth and beauty of original works, which you can't enjoy through Chinese translations.

The stories are easy for you to understand because of your familiarity with them. When you enjoy reading, your ability to understand English will also rapidly improve.

This series of **Let's Enjoy Masterpieces** is a special reading comprehension booster program, devised to improve reading comprehension for beginners whose command of English is not satisfactory, or who are elementary, middle, and high school students. With this program, you can enjoy reading masterpieces in English with fun and efficiency.

This carefully planned program is composed of 5 levels, from the beginner level of 350 words to the intermediate and advanced levels of 1,000 words. With this program's level-by-level system, you are able to read famous texts in English and to savor the true pleasure of the world's language.

The program is well conceived, composed of reader-friendly explanations of English expressions and grammar, quizzes to help the student learn vocabulary and understand the meaning of the texts, and fabulous illustrations that adorn every page. In addition, with our "Guide to Listening," not only is reading comprehension enhanced but also listening comprehension skills are highlighted.

In the audio recording of the book, texts are vividly read by professional American actors. The texts are rewritten, according to the levels of the readers by an expert editorial staff of native speakers, on the basis of standard American English with the ministry of education recommended vocabulary. Therefore, it will be of great help even for all the students that want to learn English.

Please indulge yourself in the fun of reading and listening to English through *Let's Enjoy Masterpieces*.

露意莎・梅・奧爾柯特

Louisa May Alcott
(1832–1888)

Louisa May Alcott (1832–1888), the author of *Little Women*, and her three sisters were born in Boston, a seaport and the capital of the American state of Massachusetts.

At the age of eight, she moved to nearby Concord with her family. There she spent the happiest years of her youth, even though she experienced the constant threat of poverty. The Alcotts had only a modest cottage, but the girls used a neighboring barn to perform plays that Louisa wrote.

She was educated at home and became a schoolteacher in Boston. Her first story was sold when she was twenty years old, and two years later her first full-length book was published. What pleased her the most about her writing, as she became more and more famous, was the sales of her books made her family's life more comfortable and less of a struggle. *Little Women*, published in 1869, has become one of America's classics.

About the story

Little Women is the story of the March family, a family that is used to hard work and suffering. Although Mr. March is away with the Union Army, the four sisters, Meg, Jo, Beth, and Amy and their mother keep their spirits high. Mrs. March is involved in local charity affairs, and under her influence, the girls always generously offer their help to people in need.

At a big party during the Christmas season, the March sisters meet a young man named Laurie and have a wonderful time. Because of Mr. March's injury, the sisters must face the real challenge of being independent. Things get worse when Beth contracts scarlet fever and struggles with the illness.

With the strains of separation and reunion with loved ones, plus the adventure to the outside world pursuing their careers, the March sisters become mature, gain wisdom, and find the happiness through their family life.

HOW TO USE THIS BOOK

本書使用說明

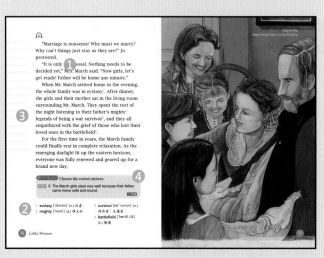

1 Original English texts

It is easy to understand the meaning of the text, because the text is rewritten according to the levels of the readers.

2 Explanation of the vocabulary

The words and expressions that include vocabulary above the elementary level are clearly defined.

3 Response notes

Spaces are included in the book so you can take notes about what you don't understand or what you want to remember.

4 Check Up

Review quizzes to check your understanding of the text.

∩ *Audio Recording*

In the audio recording, native speakers narrate the texts in standard American English. By combining the written words and the audio recording, you can listen to English with great ease.

Audio books have been popular in Britain and America for many decades. They allow the listener to experience the proper word pronunciation and sentence intonation that add important meaning and drama to spoken English. Students will benefit from listening to the recording twenty or more times.

After you are familiar with the text and recording, listen once more with your eyes closed to check your listening comprehension. Finally, after you can listen with your eyes closed and understand every word and every sentence, you are then ready to mimic the native speaker.

Then you should make a recording by reading the text yourself. Then play both recordings to compare your oral skills with those of a native speaker.

HOW TO IMPROVE
READING ABILITY
如何增進英文閱讀能力

1 *Catch key words*

Read the key words in the sentences and practice catching the gist of the meaning of the sentence. You might question how working with a few important words could enhance your reading ability. However, it's quite effective. If you continue to use this method, you will find out that the key words and your knowledge of people and situations enables you to understand the sentence.

2 *Divide long sentences*

Read in chunks of meaning, dividing sentences into meaningful chunks of information. In the book, chunks are arranged in sentences according to meaning. If you consider the sentences backwards or grammatically, your reading speed will be slow and you will find it difficult to listen to English.

You are ready to move to a more sophisticated level of comprehension when you find that narrowly focusing on chunks is irritating. Instead of considering the chunks, you will make it a habit to read the sentence from the beginning to the end to figure out the meaning of the whole.

③ *Make inferences and assumptions*

Making inferences and assumptions is part of your ability. If you don't know, try to guess the meaning of the words. Although you don't know all the words in context, don't go straight to the dictionary. Developing an ability to make inferences in the context is important.

The first way to figure out the meaning of a word is from its context. If you cannot make head or tail out of the meaning of a word, look at what comes before or after it. Ask yourself what can happen in such a situation. Make your best guess as to the word's meaning. Then check the explanations of the word in the book or look up the word in a dictionary.

④ *Read a lot and reread the same book many times*

There is no shortcut to mastering English. Only if you do a lot of reading will you make your way to the summit. Read fun and easy books with an average of less than one new word per page. Try to immerse yourself in English as often as you can.

Spend time "swimming" in English. Language learning research has shown that immersing yourself in English will help you improve your English, even though you may not be aware of what you're learning.

CONTENTS

Appendixes

Before You Read

Mr. and Mrs. March

are parents of four lovely daughters. Mrs. March takes care of the family while Mr. March serves in the Union Army during the American Civil War.

Meg

the oldest daughter, is thoughtful and considerate. She devotes herself to the family.

Jo

the second oldest daughter, is outspoken and straightforward. She enjoys writing very much.

Beth

the third oldest daughter, is quiet and tender. Beth likes to play the piano.

Amy

the youngest daughter, is a little naughty but adorable. Amy has a talent for painting.

Aunt March

Mr. March's aunt, owns a large fortune but lives a lonely life.

Laurie

the Marches' neighbor, lives with his grandfather, Mr. Laurence. Laurie is the only child in a wealthy family. He is kind and attentive.

John

Laurie's tutor, falls in love with Meg.

Chapter One

Christmas at the Marches' Home

Everything was covered with snow. The Christmas season arrived again for the girls of the March family. They longed for nice gifts, but their family's financial[1] situation was too tight to afford any.

Meg, the oldest of the four sisters, started with a sigh, "It just doesn't seem like Christmas without presents."

Amy, the youngest sister, frowned and whispered, "I am desperate[2] for colored pencils."

Jo, the second sister, said, "Honestly, I wish I didn't have to work for Aunt March, that old miser[3]."

Beth raised her eyebrows and uttered[4], "I'd like the war to end so Father can come home . . . "

---

1. **financial** [faɪˋnænʃəl] (a.) 財務的
2. **desperate** [ˋdɛspərɪt] (a.) 極度渴望的
3. **miser** [ˋmaɪzɚ] (n.) 守財奴
4. **utter** [ˋʌtɚ] (v.) 說

"Oh, sweet Beth, that's what we all want!" the other sisters declared together.

Then Jo shared her wish of becoming a writer someday. Amy was confident that she would be very rich, because she would marry a wealthy man.

Amy amused[1] her sisters further with her philosophical[2] saying, "We'll all grow up someday. We might as well know what we want."

When Mrs. March came home, the girls happily exclaimed "Mommy" and dashed[3] to the door to greet her. Mrs. March surprised the girls with a letter from their father, and they read it aloud together.

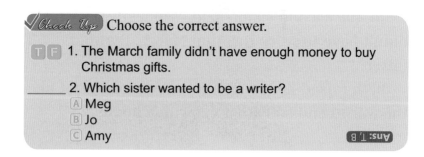

Check Up Choose the correct answer.

T F 1. The March family didn't have enough money to buy Christmas gifts.

_____ 2. Which sister wanted to be a writer?
    Ⓐ Meg
    Ⓑ Jo
    Ⓒ Amy

Ans: T, B

1. **amuse** [ə`mjuːz] (v.) 使發笑
2. **philosophical** [ˌfɪlə`sɑːfɪkl] (a.) 哲學的
3. **dash** [dæʃ] (v.) 急奔

The girls felt relieved that their father was safe and sound, but they felt sorry that he had to endure the loneliness of being separated from the family.

Soon enough, their sentimental[1] notion[2] was replaced with cheerful festivity; the girls sang Christmas carols until bedtime. As usual, Jo stayed up late writing about her fantasy world.

On the Christmas day, Jo woke up to the delightful aroma[3] of breakfast being prepared by Meg and their maid, Hannah. Mrs. March had gone out to help a German family, the Hummels.

---

1. **sentimental** [ˌsɛntəˈmɛntl̩] (a.) 多愁善感的
2. **notion** [ˈnoʊʃən] (n.) 想法
3. **aroma** [əˈroʊmə] (n.) 香味

Mrs. Hummel and her six kids had been living in harsh poverty since Mr. Hummel passed away. Beth, equipped[4] with exceptionally noble morals[5], motivated[6] the sisters to deliver[7] some food to the Hummels.

On their way back home from delivering the food, the March girls noticed that a young man and his grandfather were moving into a fine residence[8] nearby.

The old man was Mr. Laurence. Full of curiosity, the sisters chatted all night about the lonely-looking young man's background.

Check Up Choose the correct answer.

T F 3. Mr. March sent a letter home.

T F 4. Mrs. March prepared breakfast.

Ans: T, F

4. **equip** [ɪˈkwɪp] (v.) 配備；具有
5. **morals** [ˈmɔːrəlz] (n.) (pl.) 道德
6. **motivate** [ˈmoutɪveɪt] (v.) 激發
7. **deliver** [dɪˈlɪvər] (v.) 運送
8. **residence** [ˈrezɪdəns] (n.) 宅邸

4

Jo and Meg were going to attend[1] a New Year's party.

Meg was dressing up for the party. Jo was using a hot iron stick to curl Meg's hair while chatting with the other girls. Beth was glad she didn't have to socialize[2] with strangers but could stay home with Amy.

Suddenly, a burning smell caught Jo's attention. She had ruined Meg's hair. That caused quite a panic[3] until Amy decorated Meg's burnt hair with a ribbon, and Meg looked fantastic, as usual.

At the party, Meg was constantly occupied, since many young men invited her to dance. Unexpectedly, Jo bumped into the newcomer in their neighborhood, Laurie, the grandson of old Mr. Laurence. They had a wonderful time.

Alas, Meg twisted[4] her ankle and had to leave early. The sisters were thankful to Laurie, the Marches' new acquaintance[5], because he had kindly offered them a comfortable ride home in his carriage[6].

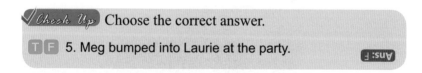

Check Up Choose the correct answer.

T F 5. Meg bumped into Laurie at the party.

Ans: F

1. **attend** [əˋtɛnd] (v.) 出席
2. **socialize** [ˋsoʃəlaɪz] (v.) 交際
3. **panic** [ˋpænɪk] (n.) 驚慌
4. **twist** [twɪst] (v.) 扭傷
5. **acquaintance** [əˋkweɪntəns] (n.) 相識的人
6. **carriage** [ˋkærɪdʒ] (n.) 馬車

Little Women

Chapter Two

🎧 5

The Drama of Daily Life

The Christmas season was over, and every day the girls would have to get up early and remain busy all day.

One morning while Meg waited for her sisters outside, Laurie walked by with another young man, John Brooke, Laurie's tutor[1]. They briefly exchanged greetings before the girls went on their way.

The March sisters had left the house, except for Beth. She was too bashful[2] to go to school. Though she had tried to attend school, her bashfulness had caused her to suffer too much.

She first did her lessons at home with her father. Even when both parents were busy, Beth proceeded[3] by herself and accomplished[4] as many lessons as she could. She also helped Hannah with cooking and kept the home neat.

Check Up Choose the correct answer.

T F 1. Beth was too shy to attend school, so she stayed home.

Ans: T

"Oh, dear, how depressing[5] it is to go back to work in the nursery[6]," sighed Meg.

"I wish it were the holidays all the time," answered Jo, yawning dismally[7]. Her job, being Aunt March's companion, wasn't fun either. The childless old lady was lame[8] and needed an active person to wait upon her.

Amy tagged along[9] with the two sisters and said, "I wish I were Beth, so I could stay home and focus on meaningful pursuits."

1. **tutor** [ˋtuːtər] (n.) 家庭教師
2. **bashful** [ˋbæʃfəl] (a.) 羞怯的
3. **proceed** [prəˋsiːd] (v.) 繼續進行
4. **accomplish** [əˋkɑːmplɪʃ] (v.) 完成
5. **depressing** [dɪˋpresɪŋ] (a.) 令人沮喪的
6. **nursery** [ˋnɜːrsəri] (n.) 托兒所
7. **dismally** [ˋdɪzməli] (adv.) 憂鬱地
8. **lame** [leɪm] (a.) 跛腳的
9. **tag along** 跟隨；緊跟

"Yeah, if you call doing housework a meaningful pursuit!" Jo said.

Jo's remark dampened[1] the thoughts in Amy's mind. "How about Laurie? Does he go to school?" questioned Amy.

"He has a tutor, remember? The guy we just met. I forgot his name," Jo uttered.

"Mr. Brooke. He said we could call him John," Meg recalled[2].

"That's right. I wonder . . ." Jo was interrupted by Amy's nearly crying tone.

"I can't go to school today if I have nothing to treat my classmates. I've been taking their treats and I owe them so much . . . "

Since Amy kept begging persistently[3], Meg finally gave her a quarter[4] to buy some treats for her schoolmates.

✓ *Check Up* Choose the correct answer.

T F   2. Jo enjoyed working as Aunt March's companion.

T F   3. Laurie didn't have to go to school because he had a tutor.

Ans: F, T

---

1. **dampen** [`dæmpən] (v.) 使消沈

2. **recall** [rɪ`kɔːl] (v.) 回想

3. **persistently** [pər`sɪstəntli] (adv.) 持續不斷地

4. **quarter** [`kwɔːrtər] (n.) 25分硬幣

Amy had a distinguished talent[1] for drawing. Her teachers complained that instead of summing up the assigned[2] mathematical work, her notebook was covered with designs.

Amy kept her academic performance up as well as she could. In school, she was well-known for her good temper and artistic appreciation[3].

Later that day, Amy came home weeping[4]. Her hands were swollen[5]. She caused quite a disturbance[6]. Amy had refused to share with her classmates the treats that she had bargained[7] for with the money Meg had given her. She'd been in a confrontation[8] with her teacher and had been punished.

1. **talent** [ˋtælənt] (n.) 才華；天分
2. **assigned** [əˋsaɪnd] (a.) 指定的
3. **appreciation** [ə͵priːʃɪˋeɪʃən] (n.) 鑑賞
4. **weep** [wiːp] (v.) 哭泣
5. **swollen** [ˋswoʊlən] (a.) 腫起來的
6. **disturbance** [dɪˋstɜːrbəns] (n.) 混亂
7. **bargain** [ˋbaːrgən] (v.) 討價還價
8. **confrontation** [͵kaːnfrənˋteɪʃən] (n.) 對抗

🎧 8

Mrs. March wrote a letter to the school expressing her disappointment and decided that Amy should stay home and let Jo become her tutor. Mrs. March even mentioned that if Jo had problems finding teaching material, she could consult[1] Laurie's tutor, Mr. Brooke.

Although Jo wasn't at all interested in being Amy's supervisor[2], she had no excuse to turn her mother down, and so she reluctantly promised her mother that she would do the tutoring.

Meg was Amy's intimate[3] and also her monitor[4], and by some strange attraction of opposites, enthusiastic Jo shared a faithful relationship with shy Beth.

Meg and Jo, the two older girls, were a great deal closer to one another, but each took one of the younger sisters under her guidance in her own way. "Playing Mother," as they called it, naturally exercised the maternal instincts[5] of these little women.

✓ *Check Up* Choose the correct answer.

T F 4. Jo promised she would tutor Amy at home.

Ans: T

1. **consult** [kənˋsʌlt] (v.) 請教
2. **supervisor** [ˋsuːpərˏvaɪzər] (n.) 監督人
3. **intimate** [ˋɪntəmət] (n.) 至交；密友
4. **monitor** [ˋmɑːnɪtər] (n.) 規勸者
5. **instinct** [ˋɪnstɪŋkt] (n.) 本能

Chapter Three

Amy's Revenge[1] and Jo's Rage[2]

For recreation[3], the March girls regularly acted in plays that Jo wrote. Laurie had recently joined the girls for several rehearsals[4] and was planning to take Jo and Meg out to a theater that night.

Amy complained, "I want to go to the theater. I never get to go anywhere."

While she was getting ready, Jo replied, "You are too little."

Amy was frustrated[5]. She argued, "I'm not too little. You are just hogging[6] Laurie. Can I go, please?"

"Amy, I'm afraid Laurie only reserved four tickets," explained Meg.

Jo continued, "Stop being annoying. It's just Meg, me, Laurie, and that dull Mr. Brooke."

1. **revenge** [rɪˋvendʒ] (n.)
   報仇；報復
2. **rage** [reɪdʒ] (n.)（一陣）狂怒
3. **recreation** [ˌrekriˋeɪʃən] (n.)
   消遣；娛樂
4. **rehearsal** [rɪˋhɜːrsəl] (n.)
   排練；試演
5. **frustrated** [ˋfrʌstreɪtɪd] (a.)
   洩氣的；挫敗的
6. **hog** [hɑːg] (v.) 霸佔

Amy begged Jo to ask Laurie for another ticket, but her request was refused. Beth offered to make some ginger tea[7] for Amy, suggesting that since Amy had a cold, she should stay home and rest.

Before leaving, Jo assigned Amy several pages of mathematical exercises to work on. Jo was quite rigid[8] about Amy's home education, and she often disciplined[9] and criticized[10] Amy for being lazy.

After the sisters left, Amy was in grave[11] misery[12] and her usual innocence had become concealed by a wicked kind of thinking.

Check Up Choose the correct answer.

T F 1. Amy felt very bad because she had to stay home.

Ans: T

7. **ginger tea** 薑茶
8. **rigid** [ˋrɪdʒɪd] (a.) 嚴格的；苛刻的
9. **discipline** [ˋdɪsɪplɪn] (v.) 懲戒
10. **criticize** [ˋkrɪtɪsaɪz] (v.) 批評
11. **grave** [ɡreɪv] (a.) 重大的
12. **misery** [ˋmɪzəri] (n.) 痛苦；悲慘

🎧 10

As John and Meg walked home a few hours later, they exchanged some of their passionate[1] ideas about plays and dramas. Laurie and Jo trailed[2] behind and couldn't help but notice some chemistry between the two. At least John's admiration for Meg was quite obvious[3].

Jo was too protective to entertain[4] the slightest possibility that her sister might couple up with John. She rudely interrupted them and pushed Meg home.

Mrs. March was still awake, and she was working in the living room when they came in. Meg and Jo gave her a brief report about their experience at the theater.

Preoccupied by a desire to do some writing, Jo excused herself and retreated[5] to her room. Jo saw Amy reading, so she asked if Amy was still moody[6]. Jo didn't get a reply.

✔ *Check Up* Choose the correct answer.

T F 2. John admitted that he had fallen in love with a ballet dancer.

T F 3. Amy was already asleep when Jo and Meg came home.

Ans: F, F

1. **passionate** [ˋpæʃənɪt] (a.)
   熱烈的
2. **trail** [treɪl] (v.) 跟在後面
3. **obvious** [ˋɑ:bvɪəs] (a.) 明顯的
4. **entertain** [͵entərˋteɪn] (v.)
   接受；考慮
5. **retreat** [ri:ˋtri:t] (v.) 撤退
6. **moody** [ˋmu:di] (a.)
   悶悶不樂的

In the bedroom, Beth had already fallen asleep. Since Jo couldn't find her manuscript[7], she wondered if Beth had borrowed it to read and had forgotten to return it. As Jo glanced over the fireplace in the room, she shockingly saw her manuscript burning inside.

The sharp screams from Jo could probably be heard from miles away, but it was too late. The fire had consumed[8] all of her writings. Amy had taken revenge by burning Jo's manuscript.

Exploding with rage, Jo dragged Amy out of her bed and angrily shook a threatening fist while she questioned her. Amy trembled[9] and was totally frightened. She uttered no defensive[10] words and silently admitted to Jo's accusation[11].

Check Up Choose the correct answer.

T F 4. Beth borrowed Jo's manuscript to read and had not yet returned it.

Ans: F

7. **manuscript** [ˈmænjuskrɪpt] (n.) 手稿；原稿
8. **consume** [kənˈsuːm] (v.) 毀滅
9. **tremble** [ˈtrembəl] (v.) 顫抖
10. **defensive** [dɪˈfensɪv] (a.) 防禦的；保衛的
11. **accusation** [ˌækjuˈzeɪʃən] (n.) 指控；指責

🎧 11

"I hate you, and I will never forgive you," Jo wept and murmured[1] repeatedly. She felt crushed[2], but instead of hitting Amy, she just kept banging[3] her own fist on the floor.

Mrs. March and Meg heard the commotion[4] and arrived presently to find things worse than they had thought. The situation was too complicated[5] to be smoothed away[6].

Meg took Amy aside while Mrs. March comforted Jo. Mrs. March hoped that Jo and Amy's relationship would soon be back in harmony[7].

Check Up Choose the correct answer.

T F 5. Jo accused Amy of burning her manuscript out of revenge.

Ans: T

---

1. **murmur** [ˋmɝːrmər] (v.) 私語;低聲說
2. **crush** [krʌʃ] (v.) 壓垮;摧毀
3. **bang** [bæŋ] (v.) 猛擊
4. **commotion** [kəˋmouʃən] (n.) 騷動
5. **complicated** [ˋkɑmplɪkeɪtɪd] (a.) 複雜的;難懂的
6. **smooth away** 消除;解決
7. **harmony** [ˋhɑːrməni] (n.) 和諧;融洽

Chapter Four

🎧12 A Woman's Duty and Beauty

Jo had not talked to Amy ever since the night they fought. One day, when Jo and Laurie ventured[1] out to skate on the frozen[2] lake, Amy followed along, even though Jo still ignored her.

Some of the ice on the lake was too thin, and it cracked[3]. Amy fell into the icy water and yelled for help. Fortunately, Jo and Laurie were close enough to rescue Amy and save her life.

This event consequently brought an end to Jo and Amy's cold war[4], and they finally made up[5].

✓*Check Up* Choose the correct answer.

T F 1. Jo and Amy began to talk to each other again only after the accident on the lake.

Ans: T

1. **venture** [ˋvɛntʃər] (v.) 冒險去……
2. **frozen** [ˋfrozən] (a.) 結冰的
3. **crack** [kræk] (v.) 破裂
4. **cold war** 冷戰
5. **make up** 和好

In the spring, the March sisters were busy helping Meg prepare to attend a party, a social occasion where the teenage dream of meeting future spouses[6] was often realized.

A matchmaker's[7] visit to the March family was a reminder[8] that it was time for Meg to look for a suitable match. The matchmaker told Mrs. March that Meg's marriage might solve the Marches' financial difficulties.

Right before leaving home, Meg could not find her party gloves[9], so she had to borrow her mother's. She couldn't help but think it would be nice to have extra pairs of gloves and perhaps it would be a good idea for her to marry a wealthy man.

Check Up Choose the correct answer.

T F 2. Meg totally rejected the idea of getting married to a wealthy man.

Ans: F

6. **spouse** [spaʊs] (n.) 配偶
7. **matchmaker** [ˋmætʃˏmeɪkər] (n.) 媒人
8. **reminder** [rɪˋmaɪndər] (n.) 提醒
9. **glove** [glʌv] (n.) 手套

Once Meg arrived at the party, she couldn't resist the luxury of putting on a rich girl's spare evening gown[1] and elaborate[2] make-up. She found out that it was enjoyable to exhibit her charm as a social butterfly.

In the meantime, Laurie was at the party and witnessed this vain[3] side of Meg. He teased[4] Meg in private for being phony[5]. Meg felt ashamed about her shallow[6] deed and asked Laurie to keep her sisters from knowing how she had behaved at the party. Ironically[7], their conversation invited the gossip of spectators[8].

✓ *Check Up* Choose the correct answer.

T F 3. The March family knew about Meg's vain behavior because of Laurie's careless mention.

Ans: F

1. **evening gown** 晚禮服
2. **elaborate** [ɪˋlæbərət] (a.) 精心製作的；精巧的
3. **vain** [veɪn] (a.) 愛虛榮的
4. **tease** [tiːz] (v.) 取笑；逗弄
5. **phony** [ˋfoʊnɪ] (a.) 虛偽的；假的
6. **shallow** [ˋʃælou] (a.) 膚淺的
7. **ironically** [aɪˋrɑːnɪklɪ] (adv.) 諷刺地
8. **spectator** [ˋspekteɪtər] (n.) 觀眾；旁觀者

Back home, Meg and Jo had a discussion with Mrs. March about how the society treated men and women differently. Meg questioned why women were often subjected to[1] criticism[2], especially women whose enjoyment included flirting[3] with other men, while men were never disgraced for doing the very same thing. Mrs. March felt sorry about the unfairness of the world.

"Indeed, men are always in a more favorable[4] position than women. Men can vote, hold property, and pursue any professions they please," asserted Mrs. March.

"However, women are prohibited[5] from doing those things. It is as if all of us women should only become housewives and focus our lives on pregnancy and motherhood," Jo protested[6].

Check Up Choose the correct answer.

T F 4. Men would not be looked down upon for flirting with women.

Ans: T

---

1. **be subjected to**
   蒙受；遭遇
2. **criticism** [ˋkrɪtɪsɪzəm] (n.)
   批評；批判
3. **flirt** [flɜːrt] (v.) 調情

4. **favorable** [ˋfeɪvərəbəl] (a.)
   贊同的；有利的
5. **prohibit** [prəˋhɪbɪt] (v.)
   禁止；阻止
6. **protest** [prəˋtest] (v.) 反對

Jo felt it was ridiculous[7] that there was no equality[8] between men and women. She thought a woman should follow her own will, regardless of the opinions of others, and never follow the herd. Meg disagreed, because she did care about others' views; she liked to look beautiful, to be praised, and to be admired.

Mrs. March told Meg that how she viewed herself was more important than what others thought. If she regarded her value merely as a decoration, then that would limit the great potential contribution she could make.

"Time erodes[9] all such superficial beauty, but the true beauty of women's wisdom and moral courage endures. Those are the merits[10] both men and women should honor the most," Mrs. March concluded.

Check Up Choose the correct answer.

T F 5. Mrs. March believed that outer beauty would not last, but inner beauty would.

Ans: T

7. **ridiculous** [rɪˋdɪkjʊləs] (a.) 荒謬的

8. **equality** [ɪˋkwɑːləti] (n.) 平等；相等

9. **erode** [ɪˋroʊd] (v.) 磨損

10. **merit** [ˋmerɪt] (n.) 價值；長處

Chapter Five

🎧15 Moody Jo and Unfortunate News

Recently, Jo was very moody and depressed[1], because Laurie was about to leave for Harvard to study for the coming semester[2]. According to Laurie's timetable[3], he had better start packing.

With Jo's companion and assistance, Laurie was bundling up his stuff in his grandfather's house. Jo kept handing Laurie bunches of books, which they had read together, for him to pack up.

Laurie addressed Jo gently, "I don't think those books are necessary to bring. After all, I won't have time to read them again."

✓ *Check Up* Choose the correct answer.

T F 1. Jo couldn't wait to say farewell to Laurie so she could make some new friends.

Ans: F

1. **depressed** [dɪˋprɛst] (a.) 沮喪的；消沉的
2. **semester** [sɪˋmɛstər] (n.) 一學期
3. **timetable** [ˋtaɪm͵teɪbəl] (n.) 時間表；課程表

"Of course not. You'll have more important things to read since you're becoming an intellectual[1]. Your peers[2] are great learners like you, climbing the ladder of the academy and eventually graduating to become scholars, which is in contrast with my probable future of becoming an amateur in some field or other," Jo replied bitterly.

She felt dreadful[3]. It seemed as if she was going to be left behind by her best friend. She continued, "I guess those books don't fit in your life any more."

Laurie countered, "Jo, nothing will change. We will still be best friends, regardless of our different future paths. Also, I feel mine is not as definite as yours, since you are always ambitious toward the future, but I am just the contrary."

✓ Check Up Choose the correct answer.

T F 2. Jo spoke bitter words to Laurie because she felt as if Laurie was leaving her behind, like those old books they had read together.

Ans: T

1. **intellectual** [ˌɪntəˈlɛktʃuəl] (n.) 知識分子
2. **peer** [pɪr] (n.) 同輩
3. **dreadful** [ˈdrɛdfəl] (a.) 糟透了的
4. **vague** [veɪg] (a.) 朦朧的

Jo's eyes covered with a vague[4] glare, unlike her usually vigorous sharpness. She uttered lifelessly, "You will be having all kinds of fascinating encounters[5] and splendid experiences in your new surroundings. And when you come back, you will already have experienced so many things or grasped so much knowledge that you'll have nothing to share with me."

"Although you are exaggerating, I must confess that there is something I know and you are unaware of, which is . . . about Meg and my former tutor, Mr. John Brooke." Laurie tried to soothe[6] Jo by diverting her attention.

Jo raised her eyebrows with a doubtful stare as she questioned Laurie, "What are you talking about? Is there some kind of hidden romance between them? I don't believe you."

Laurie responded, "Meg misplaced[7] one of her gloves, didn't she? I know that John cherishes Meg's glove and carries it with him in his pocket all the time."

Check Up Choose the correct answer.

T F 3. The information Jo didn't know but learned from Laurie was about Meg and John.   Ans: T

5. **encounter** [ɪnˈkaʊntər] (n.)
遭遇

6. **soothe** [suːð] (v.) 安慰；緩和

7. **misplace** [mɪsˈpleɪs] (v.)
隨意擱置；遺忘

As awkward as it might seem, Jo hastened home to inform Meg, or more precisely, to confront[1] her. "Don't you find it offensive[2] that John actually stole your personal belonging?"

Meg blushed[3] but didn't respond.

Then Jo continued, "Turns out it is nothing mysterious. It was John's theft of your glove."

Meg finally replied, "I really don't associate[4] John with your accusation. I think he is an honest man of maturity[5]. He must have found my glove somewhere after I lost it, and he didn't have the opportunity to return it yet."

Jo uttered promptly[6], "And now you are even defending him . . . "

✓*Check Up* Choose the correct answer.

T F 4. Meg reacted furiously when Jo accused John of being a thief.

Ans: F

1. **confront** [kən`frʌnt] (v.)
   使面對;使對質
2. **offensive** [ə`fensɪv] (a.)
   冒犯的
3. **blush** [blʌʃ] (v.) 因害羞臉紅

4. **associate** [ə`souʃi,eɪt] (v.)
   聯想
5. **maturity** [mə`turəti] (n.)
   成熟
6. **promptly** [`prɑːmptli]
   (adv.) 立即地

Meanwhile, Mrs. March hurried into the dining room and interrupted the sisters' conversation. Her voice shivered[7] as if she was about to faint at any minute. "Jo, Meg! I just received a telegram[8] . . . from Washington Hospital. Your father has been wounded."

This unfortunate news disrupted[9] everything in the March family and immediately put everyone in great stress and anxiety.

Check Up Choose the correct answer.

T F 5. The telegram Mrs. March received brought the March family a hard time.

Ans: T

7. **shiver** [ˋʃɪvər] (v.) 發抖

8. **telegram** [ˋtelɪgræm] (n.) 電報

9. **disrupt** [disˋrʌpt] (v.) 擾亂；使……中斷

Chapter Six

🎧 18

Mrs. March's Travel Plan

Mrs. March decided to visit Mr. March as soon as possible. However, the March family didn't have extra money for the train fare[1]. Since Mrs. March had already sold all of her jewelry, she sent Jo to Aunt March to borrow some money.

Meanwhile, the other sisters were preparing some stuff for Mrs. March's travel. Beth was folding Mrs. March's clothes, and Amy wanted Mrs. March to bring a blanket in case it got too cold at night.

✓ *Check Up* Choose the correct answer.

T F 1. Mrs. March could afford the train fare after having sold all of her jewelry.

Ans: F

---

1. **fare** [fer] (n.) 交通費用；車資
2. **delegate** [ˋdelɪɡeɪt] (v.) 委派某人做……

Although Mrs. March thought her daughters were mature enough to live on their own, she still instructed them on different tasks. She first delegated[2] Meg to keep a record of household finances. Then she asked Beth to make sure the poor Hummels had enough food and firewood. Mrs. March also got little Amy to promise she would be a nice girl.

In the meantime, Laurie and John visited the Marches. Laurie said, "What a pity that Mr. March has been wounded. Grandfather parceled[3] some sliced ham and some stuffed bell peppers[4] for you to enjoy on the road."

"Thank you," Mrs. March replied in gratitude[5].

Next, Meg introduced John to her mother.

Check Up Choose the correct answer.

T F 2. Mrs. March asked Beth to take care of the poor Hummels while she was away.

Ans: T

3. **parcel** [ˋpɑːrsl] (v.)
把……包起來

4. **bell pepper** 鐘型辣椒

5. **gratitude** [ˋgrætəˌtuːd] (n.)
感激之情

John politely and sincerely explained, "As Laurie no longer requires a tutor, Mr. Laurence has work for me in Washington. Because of the war, the dangers of traveling have been compounded[1] with the fears of robbery. I should volunteer to escort you there. Please let me ensure that you arrive at your destination safely. I hope you don't mind that I have made reservations for us on the next train, which will depart[2] at six this evening."

Mrs. March was overwhelmed with gratitude, since she knew how dangerous it was for a woman to travel alone. She gratefully uttered, "Mr. Brooke, how kind of you."

"Shall we get moving to the train station?" John inquired.

"Yes, but I am waiting for Jo," Mrs. March replied worriedly.

Check Up Choose the correct answer.

T F 3. As Laurie's tutor and loyal supporter, John followed Laurie to visit Mr. March in Washington.

T F 4. Mrs. March kindly rejected John because she preferred to travel alone.

Ans: F, F

1. **compound** [kɑːmˋpaʊnd] (v.) 使加重;惡化

2. **depart** [dɪˋpɑːrt] (v.) 啟程;出發

"Why is it taking Jo so long?" Amy wondered.

"Battling[3] with Aunt March for money is never easy," Meg answered.

In her hooded coat, Jo suddenly entered the front door. Exhausted from running, Jo was breathless[4] as she palmed $25 to her mother.

Mrs. March remarked unbelievably, "Aunt March is rarely so generous."

"It's not from Aunt March. I put my useless long hair into a decent usage," Jo replied as she removed her hood.

To everyone's surprise, Jo's beautiful long hair was gone.

"My goodness!" exclaimed Mrs. March.

"I didn't want to trash[5] my dignity and waste time begging Aunt March for money, so I sold my hair," Jo replied casually.

Check Up Choose the correct answer.

T F 5. Jo sold her hair so Mrs. March would be able to visit Mr. March.

Ans: T

---

3. **battle** [ˋbætl] (v.) 與……奮鬥
4. **breathless** [ˋbrεθləs] (a.) 氣喘吁吁的
5. **trash** [træʃ] (v.) 把……視為廢物

Amy let loose of her tongue, "How bold you are! Hair is the only thing that could make you qualified as beautiful . . . "

Meg hushed Amy and then asked, "Why didn't you sell the copper[1] kettle?"

"No way. We need it to boil water. It is just hair, no big deal. It will grow back, right? I can still be elegant[2], if necessary." Jo lightened[3] the serious dialog in a joking manner.

Drunk with gratefulness[4], Mrs. March finally broke into tears as her emotions aroused[5] her. She felt fortunate to have these marvelous daughters.

She hugged Jo, kissed her forehead, and said, "My sweetheart, thank you so much for your sacrifice."

The March family shed tears as they hugged each other and whispered, "May God bless us."

1. **copper** [ˋkɑːpər] (a.)
   銅的；銅製的
2. **elegant** [ˋɛligənt] (a.)
   優雅的；優美的
3. **lighten** [ˋlaɪtn] (v.)
   使明亮；照亮
4. **gratefulness** [ˋgreɪtfəlnəs] (n.)
   感謝；感激
5. **arouse** [əˋraʊz] (v.)
   使……激動

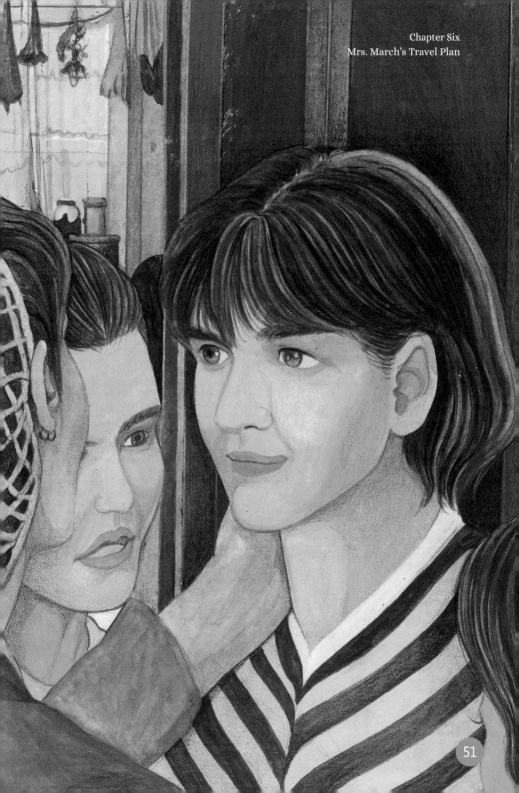

· Chapter Seven ·

🎧 The March Family's Poverty and Beth's Illness

As the March sisters were preparing breakfast, Meg informed the girls that when she was getting a pint[1] of milk at the dairy, she was told that the Marches needed to pay off their debts before they could get any more milk.

Indeed, they had been deeply in debt ever since their father left home because of the war.

Meanwhile, two biscuits[2] dropped off the tray as Amy took them out of the oven. "Oh, blast! I spoiled[3] it," Amy exclaimed.

"That's all right; we'll eat them anyway," her sisters responded.

---

1. **pint** [paɪnt] (n.) 品脫
2. **biscuit** [ˋbɪskɪt] (n.) 餅乾
3. **spoil** [spɔɪl] (v.) 糟蹋

To Jo's surprise, there were some sausages on the table. She ate one instantly, and with a peculiar look, she asked, "What a weird flavor is this?"

"It's made of pig liver[4]. Since our budget has shrunk, it's the only meat we can afford," replied Meg.

Amy suggested, "Maybe we all can become vegetarians[5]. At least I think I can survive on only wheat bread."

As devoted and charitable as she always was, Beth inquired, "What can I take to the Hummels today?"

Meg smiled and said, "Take care of your belly first. I have baked a couple of extra potatoes for them."

Even though the March sisters' financial situation had been tightened, they were still happy to help the poor.

Check Up Choose the correct answer.

T F 1. The March sisters had some bacon to go with the bread for breakfast.

Ans: F

4. **liver** ['lɪvər] (n.) 肝臟

5. **vegetarian** [ˌvedʒəˈterɪən] (n.) 素食者

22

After breakfast, Beth showed up at the Hummels' hut with potatoes as usual. Since the Hummels were new immigrants and didn't speak English, Beth couldn't understand what Mrs. Hummel was trying to tell her.

Mrs. Hummel pushed her crying baby she held in her arms to Beth and signaled[1] Beth to hold the baby.

As an unconscious reflex[2], Beth took hold of the baby, and then she realized the baby's body temperature was unusually high. Beth felt sympathetic for the poor Hummel family.

Jo went home right away after work, since Laurie should be back from school for a vacation. She picked up the weekly packet of letters from the mailbox and began to sort them out on the front porch[3]. She astonishingly found a letter addressed to her.

Check Up Choose the correct answer.

T F 2. Beth regularly visited the Hummels to give them food.

Ans: T

1. **signal** [ˋsɪɡnəl] (v.) 向……示意   3. **porch** [pɔːrtʃ] (n.)
2. **reflex** [ˋriːfleks] (n.) 反射   門廊；入口處

Eager to read it, she ripped[4] it open right then, and shortly after she yelled out as she ran into the house, "I sold my first story! Five dollars! I am an author!"

She felt she had found a secure resolution[5] to their obstacle. No one replied.

"Perhaps no one was at home," Jo thought. As she walked into the living room, she saw Beth lying on the lounge, covered with a wool blanket.

"What's wrong?" Jo asked.

Without speaking, Beth could only blink[6] her eyes. Jo touched her forehead and realized she was weakened by a high fever.

Since Mrs. March was away, the sisters didn't know what to do about Beth's illness. They only knew there was a definite connection between Beth's sickness and Mrs. Hummel's baby. With great patience, Meg was doing thorough research in Mrs. March's medical books.

Check Up Choose the correct answer.

T F 3. Beth told Jo the good news about selling her first story.

Ans: F

4. **rip** [rɪp] (v.) 拆開；撕開
5. **resolution** [ˌrezəˈluːʃən] (n.) 解決方法

6. **blink** [blɪŋk] (v.) 眨眼

23

Just then Hannah, the family's maid, arrived home from her visit to the Hummels. Sweating and panting, Hannah uttered, "Two children have been taken up to the Almighty, and both are theirs! Some neighbors say it is scarlet fever[1]."

To Jo and Meg, she continued, "You two are older and won't be harmed, since you had it when you were babies."

Then to Amy, she insisted, "But, Amy, we have to send you away. It's the only sure way of prevention from this life-threatening[2] contagion[3]."

Check Up Choose the correct answer.

Ⓣ Ⓕ 4. Hannah suggested that Amy be sent away to be safe.

Ans: T

1. **scarlet fever** 猩紅熱
2. **life-threatening** [ˋlaɪf ˋθretnɪŋ] (a.) 致命的
3. **contagion** [kənˋteɪdʒən] (n.) 傳染病

🎧 24

Later that night, Laurie rode with Amy on his carriage to Aunt March's house.

Feeling miserable, Amy cried out in despair[1]. "What a nightmare! Thanks for the rescue again." After a moment of silence, she continued, "Will I die?"

"You will be fine," Laurie replied.

Amy sighed. "I haven't even had a boyfriend yet. I can't die without being kissed."

With great affection[2], Laurie said humorously, "Don't worry! I promise to kiss you before you die."

Check Up Choose the correct answer.

T F 5. Amy was worried that she would die young.

Ans: T

1. **despair** [dɪ`spɛr] (n.) 絕望    2. **affection** [ə`fɛkʃən] (n.) 喜愛

Little Women

Chapter Eight

⌂25 Sick Beth in the Family's Intense Care

Amy had to stay with Aunt March as her companion, which used to be Jo's part-time job, but she had no idea how long she would have to stay with her aunt. She prayed for Beth every day and realized how much she loved and missed her sisters.

Surprisingly enough, Aunt March was very kind to Amy. She revealed a soft place in her old heart. She really did her best to make Amy happy.

Since Amy's previous negative impression about Aunt March was based on Jo's complaints, she realized it had evidently resulted from Jo's preconceptions[1].

Amy's motivation was simply to spend some time with Aunt March, and it worked out well. They both enjoyed each other's company.

Check Up Choose the correct answer.

T F 1. Amy, influenced by Jo, didn't like Aunt March at all.

Ans: F

Meanwhile in the Marches' house, Jo and Meg were discussing whether they should contact Mrs. March, since they scarcely knew if Beth's illness could be cured.

Meg argued that Mrs. March should stay with their father, while Jo thought that was too passive.

She was afraid even a minor illness could be fatal to Beth without Mrs. March's intensive care, which had continually saved Beth from a lung-related problem that had persisted[2] over the years.

Only Mrs. March knew how to handle it. Jo and Meg had to face the clash of competing needs between their father and sister. After considering the costly train fare necessary for Mrs. March to return, their combined dilemma appeared unsolvable[3].

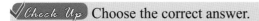 Choose the correct answer.

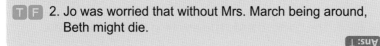

T F 2. Jo was worried that without Mrs. March being around, Beth might die.

Ans: T

1. **preconception**
   [ˌpriːkən`sepʃən] (n.)
   先入為主的偏見

2. **persist** [pər`sɪst] (v.) 持續

3. **unsolvable** [ʌn`saːlvəbl]
   (a.) 難以解決的

26

While Jo was taking care of Beth, Meg and Mr. Laurence arrived with a middle-aged man. Mr. Laurence said, "I wish my personal physician, Dr. Bangs, to conduct an overall examination of the little girl."

"Oh, my savior[1]!" Jo happily exclaimed.

She held high hope that the doctor could save Beth, as she had learned from her mother's medical journal that new technological research had allowed doctors to effectively treat different illnesses with modern inventions such as X-ray photos and manufactured pills.

After the examination, the doctor alleged[2] that he couldn't help, "Forgive me. The only thing we can do now is pray for a miracle since there is nothing to be done. It's better to send for her mother."

Check Up Choose the correct answer.

T F 3. Mr. Laurence brought his doctor to check on Beth's condition in order to treat her.

T F 4. The doctor couldn't do anything to save Beth's life.

Ans: T, T

---

1. **savior** [ˋseɪvjər] (n.) 救星　　　2. **allege** [əˋlɛdʒ] (v.) 聲稱；斷言

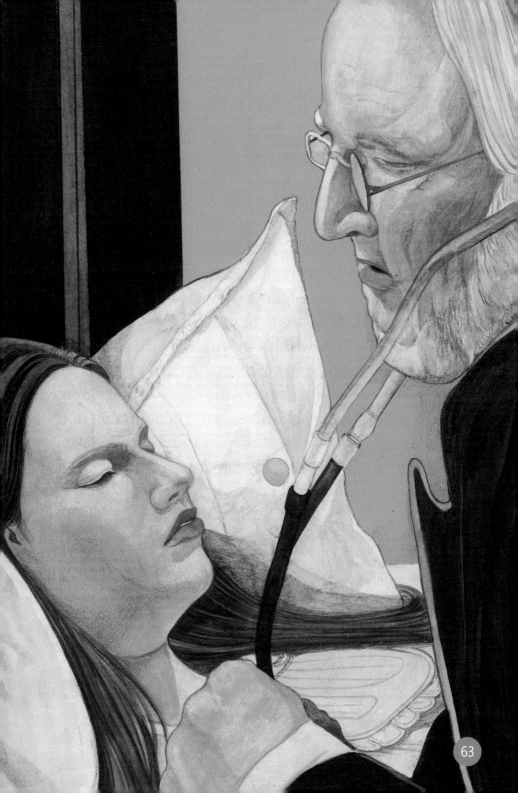

27

Upon hearing this, Jo and Meg burst into tears. Just then Laurie ran into the house and announced, "I got in touch with John in Washington and have arranged for Mrs. March to return the next morning by train."

Under the full moon, the oak tree outside the window shook from a stiff wind and cast uncanny[1] shadows on the floor. The tunes found in the calls of some owls left their signatures on Jo's mind on such a sleepless night. It almost sounded like a magical spell, Jo thought, as she spiritually and physically endowed[2] Beth with the strength of a fighter to combat[3] the illness.

She prayed to a supernatural power to heal her sister while she simultaneously[4] kept boiling hot water to pour into a container to refill the warm bags next to Beth's body. She remembered seeing Mrs. March do this before.

---

1. **uncanny** [ʌnˋkæni] (a.) 怪異的；可怕的
2. **endow** [ɪnˋdaʊ] (v.) 賦予
3. **combat** [ˋkɑːmbæt] (v.) 搏鬥；戰鬥
4. **simultaneously** [ˌsɪmlˋteɪnɪəsli] (adv.) 同時地
5. **crack** [kræk] (n.) 裂縫
6. **vinegar** [ˋvɪnɪgər] (n.) 醋
7. **kit** [kɪt] (n.) 工具箱；急救箱
8. **circulation** [ˌsɜːrkjuˋleɪʃən] (n.) 循環

Mrs. March arrived home at the crack[5] of dawn. Meg followed her into the room, where Beth was still asleep, and Jo had just woken up from a nap on the sofa. Mrs. March checked Beth's situation and swiftly rolled up her sleeves to start work.

She said, "Jo, fetch the brass basin with vinegar[6] water and a handful of clean rags. Meg, bring my kit[7]." Mrs. March calmly continued, "I must draw the fever down from her head. Let's help increase her circulation[8]."

Mrs. March moved Beth's blanket and then started rubbing Beth's limbs with hot water and vinegar until her fever finally went down.

Check Up Choose the correct answer.

T F 5. Mrs. March bathed Beth in vinegar water before taking an X-ray on her chest.

Ans: F

Chapter Nine

🎧 28 Unforgettable Christmas

As sunlight was beaming[1] through the darkest night, Beth woke up from her long sleep. The first thing she saw was her mother. The fever had drained away[2] her energy. She merely smiled and nestled up[3] in the loving arms around her. Then she slept again.

Owing to Mrs. March's nursing, Beth's face again glowed with a lively radiation over the following weeks. Her appetite[4] had increased along with her gradual recovery. Her body was still stiff and feeble[5].

Check Up Choose the correct answer.

T F 1. Beth finally recovered because of Mrs. March's nursing care.

Ans: T

1. **beam** [biːm] (v.) 照射；照耀
2. **drain away** 使變弱
3. **nestle up** 依偎
4. **appetite** [ˈæpətaɪt] (n.) 食慾
5. **feeble** [ˈfiːbl] (a.) 虛弱的；無力的

Beth needed to stretch her body, so Jo held and half carried her for a daily walk around the house. The terror of death that had been previously hovering[6] over the Marches had vanished.

As Christmas approached, the Marches' house was again filled with genuine happiness. Amy had returned home from Aunt March in time to share the letter from Mr. March with her sisters and mother.

The girls gave a lively cheer when they learned their father planned to return home before the New Year. What a blessing and encouragement for the Marches! After all the obstacles, a long-awaited[7] family reunion would soon reward the Marches' patience.

 Choose the correct answer.

T F 2. Mr. March sent home a letter to tell his family that he would soon be home.

Ans: T

6. **hover** [ˈhɑːvər] (v.) 徘徊；停留
7. **long-awaited** [ˈlɑːŋ əˈweɪtɪd] (a.) 盼望已久的

After the excitement, Jo carried Beth upstairs to rest. Laurie came to visit, bringing another piece of good news to the Marches.

"My grandfather wants to give Beth a piano that once belonged to my mother. Although it is a little old, it was well-made and is still in perfect condition," Laurie said.

"How nice of him! What a wonderful gift for Beth. Her old keyboards[1] are breaking apart. Oh, she will love it," Jo said excitedly.

"Laurie, please send my gratitude to your grandfather. I would like to invite both of you to join our Christmas dinner tomorrow," Mrs. March replied.

"Let's make the piano a surprise for Beth," Amy playfully proposed.

Check Up Choose the correct answer.

T F 3. Laurie's grandfather visited the March family to surprise Beth.

Ans: F

1. **keyboard** [ˋkiːbɔːrd] (n.) 鋼琴鍵盤

Later that evening, Laurie managed to deliver the piano to the Marches and take the old one away. The March girls, except for Beth who was asleep, cheerfully yet quietly polished[2] the piano.

They enclosed[3] the piano with a piece of beautiful cloth woven by Mrs. March and tied a bright red ribbon into a knot[4] to wrap it. The girls even furnished the room with ornaments[5] and candles. They wanted to create the most unforgettable experience for Beth.

The following day when Jo carried Beth down the staircase, everyone was assembled there to surprise Beth, including Aunt March, Laurie, and his grandfather. Beth was flooded with emotion.

Check Up Choose the correct answer.

T F 4. Beth was awake when the piano was delivered to the Marches.

Ans: F

2. **polish** [ˋpɑːlɪʃ] (v.) 擦亮
3. **enclose** [ɪnˋkloʊz] (v.) 圍住

4. **knot** [nɑːt] (n.) 結；蝴蝶結
5. **ornament** [ˋɔrnəmənt] (n.) 裝飾物；飾品

🎧 30

When she unwrapped[1] the piano, tears flowed down her cheeks. She was so deeply moved that she couldn't verbalize[2] her thankfulness. She slowly walked to the piano and stroked[3] a few keys, and then she started playing.

All of her tender feelings were expressed in the delicate musical notes. As if it was magnetic, the listeners were instantly captivated[4] and drowned in her divine grace. The Marches and their delighted guests sang in glorious chorus. They circulated around the room and greatly enjoyed a casual dance.

Check Up Choose the correct answer.

T F 5. Beth was too weak to play piano, so she expressed her gratitude in words.

Ans : F

1. **unwrap** [ʌn`ræp] (v.)
   解開；打開
2. **verbalize** [`vɜːbl͵laɪz] (v.)
   以語言描述

3. **stroke** [stroʊk] (v.)
   敲（琴鍵）
4. **captivate** [`kæptɪveɪt] (v.)
   使著迷

Chapter Ten

〔31〕 Meg's Future and a Family Reunion

Echoes of the melody Beth had played on the piano were still vivid[1] the day after Christmas. Because of Mr. March's eventual return, the festive[2] atmosphere was swelling for the Marches.

In the afternoon, Mrs. March and Meg were preparing dinner in the kitchen. Meg told her mother of John's wedding proposal[3].

Mrs. March said to Meg, "I thought you would have a long engagement[4]. I expected at least three years would pass before your marriage."

Jo overheard the conversation as she walked into the kitchen, and she was very upset at the prospect of losing her sister.

---

1. **vivid** [`vɪvɪd] (a.) 強烈的
2. **festive** [`fɛstɪv] (a.) 節日的;歡樂的
3. **proposal** [prə`pozl] (n.) 求婚
4. **engagement** [ɪn`ɡeɪdʒmənt] (n.) 訂婚

She interfered by interrogating[5] Meg, "You mean you are going to marry Mr. Brooke? He is absolutely boring."

"John has been very genial and attentive. He went to visit your father in the hospital every day," Mrs. March defensively clarified.

Jo casually expressed her dislike of John, "Meg, can't you at least marry someone amusing[6]? Or at least, someone rich, if not amusing?" Jo then turned to Mrs. March, "Mother, you can't just let her get married to whoever proposes to her. He is too poor to give Meg a good life!"

Meg finally said, "I am fond of Mr. Brooke. He is a good man with a mild temper. He is tender, kind, and serious. And I am not afraid of being poor."

✓Check Up Choose the correct answer.

T F 1. The March family was delighted to prepare Meg's wedding.

T F 2. Mrs. March disagreed with Jo and spoke up for John.

T F 3. Jo suspected that John's personality would be too violent for Meg.

Ans: F, T, F

---

5. **interrogate** [ɪnˈterəgeɪt] (v.) 質問

6. **amusing** [əˈmjuːzɪŋ] (a.) 有趣的；好玩的

"Indeed, money is important, but I hope my girls will never feel the need of it too bitterly and have to surrender the true meanings of life," explained Mrs. March.

"I would like to know that John has a concrete financial grounding[1], which allows him to have a sufficient income to keep free from debt and make Meg comfortable. I'm not ambitious for a splendid fortune, a fashionable position, or fame for my girls. If social status and money parallel[2] with love and virtue, I would be happy to accept them gratefully."

1. **grounding** [`graʊndɪŋ] (n.) 基礎
2. **parallel** [`perəlel] (v.) 與……同時發生

"But I know through experience that tons of happiness can be harbored[3] in a plain little cabin that is your shelter, and nothing can harm you there. I am content to see Meg begin humbly. My prediction is that she will be rich with her possession of a good man's heart and be the nursing mother of their children. Cultivating[4] the well of joy, accessing the fountain of inspiration, and keeping the ingredients for happiness all around are more worthwhile than having money."

"So you don't mind that John is poor?" Meg asked in a flush.

"No, but I would rather he had a house," Mrs. March replied.

Check Up Choose the correct answer.

T F 4. According to Mrs. March, Meg would be happy as long as she possessed a great fortune.

Ans: F

3. **harbor** [ˋhɑːrbər] (v.) 避入安全地
4. **cultivate** [ˋkʌltəveɪt] (v.) 培養；培育

"Marriage is nonsense! Why must we marry? Why can't things just stay as they are?" Jo protested.

"It is only a proposal. Nothing needs to be decided yet," Mrs. March said. "Now girls, let's get ready! Father will be home any minute."

When Mr. March arrived home in the evening, the whole family was in ecstasy[1]. After dinner, the girls and their mother sat in the living room surrounding Mr. March. They spent the rest of the night listening to their father's mighty[2] legends of being a war survivor[3], and they all empathized with the grief of those who lost their loved ones in the battlefield[4].

For the first time in years, the March family could finally rest in complete relaxation. As the emerging daylight lit up the eastern horizon, everyone was fully renewed and geared up for a brand new day.

Check Up Choose the correct answer.

T F 5. The March girls slept very well because their father came home safe and sound.

Ans: T

---

1. **ecstasy** [`ɛkstəsi] (n.) 狂喜
2. **mighty** [`maɪti] (a.) 偉大的
3. **survivor** [sər`vaɪvər] (n.) 倖存者；生還者
4. **battlefield** [`bætlfiːld] (n.) 戰場

Chapter Eleven

A Wedding and a Rejected Proposal

Time flew by so fast. Four years later, Meg and John got married on a day when the long-stem roses growing on the porch awoke bright and early in the morning. Meg looked very much like a rose herself. "I don't want an extravagant[1] wedding but only want to be surrounded by those whom I love, and to them I wish to look and be my familiar self," Meg told her sisters and mother.

So she made her wedding gown herself, stitching exquisite[2] lace onto the collar and the circular edge of a skirt with white threads.

Check Up Choose the correct answer.

T F 1. Meg decided to borrow a wedding dress for her wedding.

Ans: F

---

1. **extravagant** [ɪk`strævəgənt] (a.) 奢侈的;浪費的
2. **exquisite** [ɪk`skwɪzɪt] (a.) 精緻的

The outdoor setting perfectly matched the glory of the moment when Meg and John were united. An arch made of wildflowers and pine needles was erected on the lawn. It served as a monument to celebrate the first wedding for the March Family.

A flood of joy flourished among all of the guests, who scattered[3] around the garden and came forth to congratulate the bride[4] and groom[5].

Jo had learned to carry herself with ease, if not grace. There was a fresh color in her cheeks and a soft glitter[6] in her eyes. Today only appeasing[7] words fell from her usually sharp tongue.

Check Up Choose the correct answer.

T F 2. The guests stood in rows in order to greet the bride and groom.

Ans: F

3. **scatter** [`skætər] (v.) 分散
4. **bride** [braɪd] (n.) 新娘
5. **groom** [grʊm] (n.) 新郎

6. **glitter** [`glɪtər] (n.) 閃光；閃耀
7. **appeasing** [ə`piːzɪŋ] (a.) 緩和的

🎧 35

Beth had grown slender, pale, and quieter than ever. Even though her health was never fully recovered, she seldom complained and always spoke hopefully of "being better soon."

Amy was considered "the gem of the family," for at sixteen she had the air and bearing of a charming woman. From the lines of her figure to the motion of her hands, her unconscious yet harmonious[1] way was attractive to many people.

Mr. and Mrs. March were so proud of their daughters. They insisted that only the best men deserved to become their daughters' husbands.

Check Up Choose the correct answer.

T F 3. Although Beth didn't fully recover, she rarely complained.

Ans: T

---

1. **harmonious** [hɑːrˋmouniəs] (a.) 和諧的

After Meg and John's wedding, Jo and Laurie went for a walk on a forest trail.

Laurie sighed as a thin mist rolled into the valley, "Why can't I do what I want? Like being a musical composer?"

"Who is forbidding you?" Jo asked.

"After I become a graduate, Grandfather wants me to go to Europe to study business and eventually become an economist," Laurie replied.

"Don't you think you should decide your own future?" Jo wondered.

Check Up Choose the correct answer.

T F 4. Laurie's grandfather would support him to study abroad, but not as a musician.

Ans: T

36

"I must obey Grandfather, although indeed, when thinking about my future, I can't imagine my future without you. I think we should get married." Laurie spoke firmly as he kneeled[1] down, but Jo shook her head and said, "Laurie, we are best friends. You should know that I have no interest in being a wife!"

"Grandfather is the founder of a trade company with worldwide branches. We can travel everywhere we want," Laurie continued. "One day, I will inherit[2] all of the family's wealth, and you can have everything you have always been denied."

"I am not worthy, Laurie," Jo replied with determination. "We always argue because of the similarity in our personalities. I don't think it will work."

"I can be reformed[3], and I promise that I will never argue with you." Laurie insisted on swaying[4] her.

---

1. **kneel** [niːl] (v.) 跪下
2. **inherit** [ɪnˋhɛrɪt] (v.) 繼承
3. **reform** [rɪˋfɔːrm] (v.) 改正；改過
4. **sway** [sweɪ] (v.) 使動搖；影響

37

"I think the real love should stem from unfeigned[1] friendship like ours. If only you accept my proposal, the wedding date can be postponed[2] for as long as you wish."

"I am sorry, Laurie. I can't," Jo finally uttered.

Jo's feedback[3] was like a fierce thunderstorm that suddenly clouded Laurie's eyes. He ran away like a wounded bull, while Jo remained motionless as a log. The rays from the setting sun shined through the woods with a deadly quietness. No one knew if this would be the end of Laurie and Jo's relationship, but nothing would ever remain the same again.

✔ *Check Up* Choose the correct answer.

T F 5. Jo would only consider the wedding proposal if Laurie could postpone the wedding date.

Ans: F

1. **unfeigned** [ʌnˋfeɪnd] (a.) 不虛偽的；真誠的

2. **postpone** [poʊstˋpoʊn] (v.) 延期

3. **feedback** [ˋfiːdbæk] (n.) 回應

Chapter Twelve

🎧38 Unexpected Changes

Amy has been experimenting and drilling on every form of paintings. Her early sketches[1] portrayed an exceedingly[2] regular amateur quality. She made great progress, and her work had already won several prizes in art contests.

Amy then devoted herself to the finest pen-and-ink[3] drawings, in which she showed such taste and skill that her work proved both pleasant and profitable.

She designed posters for shops and theaters as a means to make money to afford more art accessories and also to frame her pictures as gifts for her family and friends.

Check Up Choose the correct answer.

T F 1. Amy spent a great deal of time practicing painting and had gained some recognition.

Ans: T

---

1. **sketch** [sketʃ] (n.) 速寫；素描
2. **exceedingly** [ɪkˈskiːdɪŋli] (adv.) 非常；特別
3. **pen-and-ink** (a.) 用鋼筆描繪的

Nothing could ever discourage Amy's aesthetic[4] expression. Even when the paint carelessly spilled[5] on the canvas[6], she could still make interesting abstract patterns.

If the weather permitted, she would go out and sit on the damp grass for hours, painting landscapes.

As Aunt March's companion, Amy regularly read books out loud to her aunt, which broadened her knowledge of history and art.

After Meg's wedding, Aunt March had a discussion with Mr. and Mrs. March about Amy's future.

"I think it would be very beneficial[7] for Amy to go to art school in Europe," suggested Aunt March. "She can receive systematic training from the most progressive teachers in the world. Also, she can explore working in clay, pottery, and sculpture." Aunt March made her point earnestly.

"But, it is too costly!" Mr. and Mrs. March said.

4. **aesthetic** [es`θetɪk] (a.)
   美感的；藝術的
5. **spill** [spɪl] (v.) 濺出
6. **canvas** [`kænvəs] (n.)
   油畫布；帆布
7. **beneficial** [ˌbenɪ`fɪʃəl] (a.)
   有助益的

🎧 39

"I will be more than happy to be her sponsor[1], since I have always wanted to go to Europe and am enjoying her companionship," Aunt Match continued. "Not to mention, it is getting harder and harder to find a good husband here nowadays. But in Europe, her chances of finding someone will be multiplied."

Mr. and Mrs. March looked at each other and both agreed that Aunt March was right.

Shortly after sunset, when Amy was still excited about Aunt March's generous offer to sponsor her study in Europe, Jo came home with a miserable look. "What's wrong?" Amy asked.

As Beth hugged Jo, Jo dissolved[2] into tears saying, "I refused Laurie's proposal."

Check Up Choose the correct answer.

T F 2. Aunt March believed that Amy might meet her future husband while studying abroad.

Ans: T

1. **sponsor** [`spɑːnsər] (n.) 贊助者

2. **dissolve** [dɪ`zɑːlv] (v.) 軟化

89

"I'm sure you can take it back. It's just a misunderstanding, right?" Amy tried to comfort Jo.

"No, my conscience knows what I really want, and I couldn't see myself as his wife. He must hate me so much that we can never face each other again. I just have to get away." Jo cried helplessly.

"Aunt March is going to Europe," Amy said.

"Europe! That's ideal! I'll put up with anything to go!" Jo responded straightaway[1].

"But Aunt March has asked me to go with her. Because of the immigration law, she can only bring one companion. Well, I am her companion now . . . " Amy replied with a slight feeling of guilt. "But perhaps she wouldn't mind if you stay at her mansion, while we are gone." As Amy finished speaking, Jo felt even more dispirited[2].

Check Up Choose the correct answer.

[T][F] 3. Jo sadly confessed to her sisters that she had turned down Laurie's wedding proposal.

[T][F] 4. Out of sympathy, Amy decided that Jo should go to Europe with Aunt March.

Ans: 3. T; 4. F

---

1. **straightaway** [ˌstreɪtəˈweɪ] (adv.) 立刻；馬上

2. **dispirited** [dɪˈspɪrɪtɪd] (a.) 氣餒的

"Of course Aunt March prefers Amy over me," Jo complained to her mother that night. "I'm ugly and inept[3] as her companion. I always say the wrong things. I turned down a perfect marriage proposal and hurt my best friend. Mom, I love our home, but I can't stand being here! I am striving for some kind of change."

"Jo, you have so many extraordinary gifts. How can you anticipate living an ordinary life?" Mrs. March said with an encouraging smile.

"You are ready to go out and find a good use for your talent, although I will miss you very much. Go, and embrace[4] your liberty and see what wonderful things come of it."

A week later, Mrs. March made arrangements for Jo to leave home. It would be Jo's first time to be away from home.

✓ *Check Up* Choose the correct answer.

T F 5. Mrs. March hoped that Jo could live a normal life and be a housewife.

Ans: F

3. **inept** [ɪ`nept] (a.) 笨拙的
4. **embrace** [ɪm`breɪs] (v.) 擁抱；欣然接受

· Chapter Thirteen ·

🎧41 Jo's New Life in the City of New York

Mrs. March's friend in New York, Mrs. Kirke, had gladly accepted Jo to tutor her daughters. The teaching job would render[1] Jo independent, and her leisure time might be made profitable by writing.

Jo liked the prospect and was eager to go, for the home nest had become like a small greenhouse[2], too confining for her restless nature and too protective for her adventurous spirit.

✔*Check Up* Choose the correct answer.

[T][F] 1. Jo would need financial support from her family while she lived in New York.

Ans: F

---

1. **render** [ˋrɛndɚ] (v.)
   使變得；使處於某種狀態

2. **greenhouse** [ˋgriːnhaʊs]
   (n.) 溫室

When she arrived, Jo was warmly greeted by Mrs. Kirke. "Now, my dear, make yourself at home," Mrs. Kirke said as she hugged Jo in a motherly way. "As the keeper of this inn, I'm on the move from morning till night. My mind can now rest at ease since I know the children are safe with you. There are always some pleasant people in the house if you feel sociable[3]. And your evenings are always free."

As they came to a room at the rear[4] of the hallway, Mrs. Kirke continued, "Come to me if anything goes wrong. My room is always open to you, and your own shall be as comfortable as I can make it. There is a sack of clean linens for you. Now I must run to deal with the hiring of some cleaners to staff the vacant[5] positions."

She bustled off, leaving Jo to settle by herself in the new place with a sense of privacy that she had never had before. Later that night, Jo wrote a letter home.

Check Up Choose the correct answer.

T F 2. Mrs. Kirke operated an inn and was busy all day long.

Ans: T

3. **sociable** [`souʃəbəl] (a.) 好交際的;善交際的

4. **rear** [rɪr] (n.) 後面;後部

5. **vacant** [`veɪkənt] (a.) 空缺的

42

Dear Mom and Beth,

Mrs. Kirke welcomed me so kindly that I felt at home right away, even in this big house full of strangers. My room has a nice table next to a sunny window, where I can write whenever I like. The marble[1] floor feels cold, so I placed Mom's handmade rug down, and it does the magic.

The nursery where I teach is a pleasant room next to Mrs. Kirke's private parlor[2], and the two little girls are lovely children. As a newcomer to the big city of New York, I must confess that I find myself feeling strange amid such a crowd.

Common people, naval[3] officers, sailors, and immigrants of all nationalities voyage worldwide with loads of cargo[4] to arrive at the home of the Statue of Liberty. They all flood into this urban jungle made of concrete. Nothing here resembles our little town of Concord.

Check Up Choose the correct answer.

T F 3. To Jo, the atmosphere of New York City was quite different from that of her hometown.

Ans: T

1. **marble** [ˋmɑːrbl] (a.) 大理石的
2. **parlor** [ˋpɑːrlər] (n.) 客廳；起居室
3. **naval** [ˋneɪvl] (a.) 海軍的
4. **cargo** [ˋkɑːrgou] (n.) 貨物

The café in Mrs. Kirke's inn is always jammed with[1] inhabitants during mealtimes. I was told that their pork chop with special sauce is really tasty. So I tried it and totally agree. The large portion makes it the best bargain around. No wonder Mrs. Kirke suggested I have my meals early to avoid the long queue[2].

Mrs. Kirke believes that I am here for "a period of sensational[3] experience before surrendering to an inevitable marital[4] fate." There is surely no lack of "sensational experience" of every kind available in such a city, but I hope that any experience I gain here will be strictly literary and as productive as possible. As I believe that my pen is mightier than any sword, I am zealous[5] to offer my contribution to humanity as a great writer.

Love,

Jo

√Check Up Choose the correct answer.

T F 4. Jo thought the café in the inn was not too expensive and delicious, but it rarely gets full.

T F 5. Jo expected the coming days in New York could enrich her creativity in writing.

Ans: F, T

---

1. **jammed with** 擠滿
2. **queue** [kjuː] (n.) 行列；隊伍
3. **sensational** [senˋseɪʃənl] (a.) 感覺的；知覺的
4. **marital** [ˋmærɪtl] (a.) 婚姻的
5. **zealous** [ˋzeləs] (a.) 積極的；熱情的

 Jo's New Friend

One morning, when Jo was having her breakfast, she saw a gentleman come along and help an elder servant to move a weighty tray of dirty dishes to the rear kitchen of the café. She remembered her father's frequent saying, "Trifles[1] show character."

When she mentioned the event to Mrs. Kirke that evening, she laughed and replied, "That must have been Mr. Bhaer; he's always doing things of that sort."

Today, Jo arranged an appointment with a publisher as an endeavor[2] to initiate her career. She had edited some sample chapters to bring along with an outline[3] of all her stories.

---

1. **trifle** [ˈtraɪfl] (n.) 瑣事；小事
2. **endeavor** [ɪnˈdɛvər] (n.) 努力；盡力
3. **outline** [ˈaʊtlaɪn] (n.) 提綱；要點

However, the publisher didn't show much interest in her stories, "Witches, knights, and furious beasts? I don't want to offend you, Miss March, but perhaps you should try those women's magazines. Our readers don't have time to dive into[1] fairy tales anymore." Jo was frustrated by the publisher's comment and left at once.

Wandering on a crowded avenue[2], Jo bumped into[3] a man and her manuscripts fell all over the muddy ground. "My apologies!" said the man, with a familiar grin.

"I've seen you helping out, doing manual labor in the café," Jo exclaimed as she recognized that man was Mr. Bhaer.

Check Up Choose the correct answer.

T F 1. The publisher thought Jo's stories were appropriate for his target readers.

T F 2. On the street, Jo accidentally met the man she had noticed earlier in the café.

Ans: F, T

1. dive into 投入；沉浸
2. avenue [ˈævənuː] (n.) 大街；大道
3. bump into 無意中遇到；撞上某人

46

"Oh, yes, I remember you too. We stay in the same inn. I am so sorry for this. Please join me at my place for coffee. Let me clean up and dry off your papers!" Mr. Bhaer proposed with a charming foreign accent and courtesy[1]. Jo merrily accepted.

"You know that when I first saw you, I thought . . . 'Ah! She is a writer!'" Mr. Bhaer said.

"What made you think so?" Jo asked.

He hinted that her fingers stained[2] with ink marks were the characteristic trait of a writer. He then poured coffee into two mugs and brought one for Jo. She had a sip but it almost spilled out. "You are far from home, Miss March? Do you miss your family?" Mr. Bhaer asked.

"Very much, especially my sisters and Laurie."

"She is your girlfriend?" Mr. Bhaer wondered.

"No, he is a good friend. We are neighbors."

Check Up Choose the correct answer.

T F 3. Someone told Mr. Bhaer that Jo was a writer.

Ans: F

---

1. **courtesy** [ˋkɜːrtəsi] (n.) 禮貌　　2. **stain** [steɪn] (v.) 沾汙；染色

After Jo's answer, there was an abrupt[3] silence until Mr. Bhaer broke the ice[4] by asking, "Do you like your coffee?"

"Oh . . . it's very strong, but I like it," Jo replied with a smile.

Jo looked around and lauded[5], "So many books!"

"I sold everything else for my passport and the boat fare to get here, except for my books," Mr. Bhaer said.

"Since you seem well-educated, let me guess, are you a librarian, chemist, or perhaps a psychologist?" Jo asked.

"In Berlin, I was a lecturer[6] and professor of philosophy at the university," he replied. "Here I am just a humble tutor who substitutes when needed."

"And a philosopher?" Jo added.

He grinned and handed Jo a book, "My book, published in German."

Check Up Choose the correct answer.

T F 4. It is not clear if Mr. Bhaer was a radical communist when he was in Berlin.

Ans: T

3. **abrupt** [ə`brʌpt] (a.) 突然的

4. **break the ice** 打破沉默
   （找話題說）

5. **laud** [lɔːd] (v.) 讚美

6. **lecturer** [`lɛktʃərər] (n.) 講師

47

Jo looked at the book briefly and asked, "Is there an English translation available?"

"Perhaps we can work in collaboration to translate it some day," he said.

Nodding her approval, Jo asked curiously, "Will you be returning to Berlin?"

"I don't think so. I have no family there anymore," he replied.

Later that night, Jo was writing home.

Dear Mom and Beth,

I had a quiet evening chatting with my new friend. I am grateful that I finally made a friend in New York. He is exceptionally kind and dynamic[1], and his wit[2] provides me the utmost amusement. I will keep a journal-letter and send it once a week. Goodnight for now, and more tomorrow.

Love,
Jo

Check Up Choose the correct answer.

T F 5. Jo wrote her family a letter to share her satisfaction that she finally made her first friend in the new environment.

Ans: T

1. **dynamic** [daɪˋnæmɪk] (a.) 有活力的
2. **wit** [wɪt] (n.) 機智;風趣

Chapter Fifteen

🎧 48

New Impressions Unfold

. . . He is as poor as one might imagine a philosopher to be. Yet, as the weeks go by, I see that he is unfailingly[1] generous to all of us who live in the house . . .

Love,
Jo

Since writing home became Jo's routine, she couldn't help but realize that Mr. Bhaer played a major role in her letters. She felt that she had to disguise[2] herself by adding things such as seeing women with high heels climbing up steep stairs, and the increasing cases of broken homes in New York City, which had the highest divorce rate in the nation.

Check Up Choose the correct answer.

T F 1. Jo thought that she shouldn't write only about Mr. Bhaer in her letters home, so she also wrote about other events. **Ans: T**

---

1. **unfailingly** [ʌnˈfeɪlɪŋli] (adv.)
   無窮盡地

2. **disguise** [dɪsˈgaɪz] (v.)
   偽裝;掩飾

Even though Jo was certain about the attraction between her and Mr. Bhaer, she rather enjoyed simply being friends with him for now.

Meanwhile, a parallel[3] story unfolded[4] in continental Europe where Amy was occupied with artistic drills.

Her paintings captivated[5] the most tranquil scenery she came across while strolling along paths in the gardens of palms, flowers, and tropical shrubs. She effortlessly captured the majesty[6] of nature, from rays flashing through the dense clouds to a flock of birds flying by a calm mirror-like lake.

Amy also found the parades[7] in town fascinating. One day she was trying to paint some bright costumes made of feathers and fur that presented the spectacle of gay spirits in a carnival[8].

Check Up Choose the correct answer.

T F 2. Capturing natural landscapes always annoys Amy because she prefers indoor activities.

Ans: F

3. **parallel** [ˈpærəlel] (a.) 平行的
4. **unfold** [ʌnˈfoʊld] (v.) 展開
5. **captivate** [ˈkæptɪveɪt] (v.) 使著迷

6. **majesty** [ˈmædʒəsti] (n.) 雄偉；壯麗
7. **parade** [pəˈreɪd] (n.) 遊行
8. **carnival** [ˈkɑːrnɪvl] (n.) 嘉年華會

49

A young man walked slowly through the crowd with his hands behind him and a somewhat absent-minded expression. He looked like an Italian, was dressed like an Englishman, and carried out the persona[1] of a liberal American.

Although there were plenty of pretty faces to admire, he seemed not to notice any of them until his eyes fell on Amy, who was concentrating on her painting. He stared at her for a moment, and then his whole face lit up. He hurried to her side and patted her on the shoulder.

"Oh, Laurie, I can't believe you are here? I thought you'd never come!" cried Amy. Her paintbrushes[2] dropped from her lap as she stood up to hug him.

"I was detained[3] on the way, but I promised to visit you, and so here I am."

✓ *Check Up* Choose the correct answer.

T F 3. A young man noticed Amy but soon walked away without interrupting her.

Ans: F

1. **persona** [pər`sonə] (n.)
   人物；角色

2. **paintbrush** [`peɪntbrʌʃ] (n.)
   畫筆

3. **detain** [dɪ`teɪn] (v.) 使耽擱

50

Amy watched him closely and felt a new sort of shyness steal over her. For he was changed, and she could not find that once merry-faced boy she had left behind in this moody-looking man in front of her.

Although he was handsomer than ever, now that the flush of pleasure at meeting her was over, he looked tired and spiritless[1].

Laurie's visit extended from a week to a month. He was tired of wandering about alone, and Amy's familiar presence seemed to add a homelike charm to the foreign scenes.

Check Up Choose the correct answer.

T F 4. After a halt in his journey, Laurie finally arrived to visit Amy as he had promised.

Ans: T

1. **spiritless** [ˋspɪrɪtləs] (a.) 沮喪的

He brought her a heap of gifts, ranging from custom-made to high-end brands, and took her to see orchestras[2] and operas. However, what bothered Amy most was that he talked and behaved out of full boast[3] without any moderate manners.

She was afraid that Laurie had become a slave to material possessions. However, she was a little terrified of disputing[4] with him. Amy was afraid that arguing with Laurie would only upset him and put him into further demoralization[5].

Contemplating[6] on how to express herself with accuracy, Amy realized the affection between her and Laurie had obviously multiplied and become interwoven into an unsolvable and unspeakable[7] complex.

Check Up Choose the correct answer.

T F 5. Amy bravely expressed how she felt about Laurie and asked him to leave her alone.

Ans: F

2. **orchestra** [ˋɔːrkɪstrə] (n.) 管絃樂隊

3. **boast** [boʊst] (n.) 自吹自擂

4. **dispute** [dɪˋspjuːt] (v.) 起爭執

5. **demoralization** [dɪˌmɔːrələˋzeɪʃən] (n.) 墮落

6. **contemplate** [ˋkɑːntəmpleɪt] (v.) 仔細思考

7. **unspeakable** [ʌnˋspiːkəbl] (a.) 無法以言語表達的

Chapter Sixteen

Transcendence Through Immortal Love

When Jo came home in the springtime, she was struck by the changes in Beth. No one seemed aware of the changes because they had come too gradually to startle[1] those who saw her daily. Nevertheless, to eyes sharpened by absence, Jo felt a heavy weight in her heart when she saw her sister's face.

There was a strange and transparent look about it, as if the individuality was being slowly stripped away, and the immortal[2] essence was barely shining through the frail[3] flesh with an indescribably but pathetic beauty. Jo saw and felt it, but said nothing at the time.

✓ Check Up Choose the correct answer.

T F 1. The changes in Beth were too gradual for those who saw her daily to observe.

Ans: T

1. **startle** [`stɑːrtl] (v.)
   使驚嚇；使嚇一跳

2. **immortal** [ɪˋmɔːrtl] (a.)
   永世的；不朽的

3. **frail** [freɪl] (a.) 身體虛弱的

The first impression soon lost much of its power, for Beth seemed happy. No one appeared to doubt that she was getting better or was alerted that she was actually getting worse.

Jo returned to New York and injected[4] her writing with a new style. Using the newspapers and various references stacked on her desk, Jo researched the headlines, scanning to seek intriguing[5] stories of criminals to pad[6] her stories.

Besides drafting new sample chapters, Jo deleted those unrealistic imaginative elements before scheduling to meet with the publisher. The publisher's comments were positive, and Jo was offered a deal.

She immediately initialed a memorandum[7] that summarized the story outline and the deadline for her work.

Check Up Choose the correct answer.

T F 2. The publisher liked Jo's new writing style and decided to work with her.

Ans: T

4. **inject** [ɪnˋdʒekt] (v.) 投入；注入

5. **intriguing** [ɪnˋtriːgɪŋ] (a.) 有趣的

6. **pad** [pæd] (v.) 填塞；襯填

7. **memorandum** [ˌmeməˋrændəm] (n.) 備忘錄

Several weeks later, Jo finished most of her writing and shared it with Mr. Bhaer for his constructive critique[1] before her final revision.

"Writing is not simply putting verbs, nouns, adjectives, and conjunctions[2] together in correct grammar," Mr. Bhaer said bluntly[3]. "I must ask why you chose to write about ignorance instead of lighting up the darkness with the torch of truth? You should be writing from how you were reared[4], from the innermost of your soul. Otherwise, it is not worth a damn."

What a humiliating punch[5] to Jo's self-esteem! She felt like a dump[6].

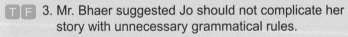

✓ Check Up Choose the correct answer.

T F 3. Mr. Bhaer suggested Jo should not complicate her story with unnecessary grammatical rules.

Ans: F

1. **critique** [krɪˋtiːk] (n.)
   評論；批評
2. **conjunction**
   [kənˋdʒʌŋkʃən] (n.) 連接詞

3. **bluntly** [ˋblʌntli] (adv.)
   直率地
4. **rear** [rɪr] (v.) 撫養
5. **punch** [pʌntʃ] (n.) 痛擊

"This is what I write, and I am sorry if it fails to live up to[7] your high standards." After uttering her feelings, Jo's tears tumbled out of her eyes. She went straight back to her room and did not show up for dinner.

Around midnight, Mrs. Kirke knocked on her door and delivered a tragic telegram that punched her once more. It said, "Beth is very ill. Come home immediately." Jo's heart was frozen.

She prayed for God's mercy to spare[8] her beloved sister, and she left for home at the crack of dawn.

Check Up Choose the correct answer.

T F 4. Jo left for home because Mr. Bhaer's criticism of her writing was too harsh to bear.

Ans: F

6. **dump** [dʌmp] (n.) 沮喪

7. **live up to** 實踐；不辜負

8. **spare** [sper] (v.) 饒恕

"Oh Beth! I love you more than anyone in the world. You must live on!" said Jo as she lay down beside her sister.

"Death can't part us, and I don't fear it any longer," Beth addressed Jo weakly. "Take care of our parents for me, and if it's hard to work alone, remember that my love will always be with you. Love is the only thing that we can carry with us to the grave, and it makes the going easier."

At Beth's memorial[1] service, she looked as if she were asleep. The sorrow of her departure would soon be transcended[2] because of Meg's pregnancy. Not only was the new life on the way to the March family, but Amy would also return with another surprise soon.

Check Up Choose the correct answer.

T F 5. The Marches' sorrow at Beth's death would soon be replaced by some good news.

Ans: T

1. **memorial** [məˋmɔːrɪəl] (a.) 追悼的；紀念的
2. **transcend** [trænˋsend] (v.) 超越

·Chapter Seventeen·

🎧54 Old Memories and New Inspiration

Jo had already sent Amy a letter to inform her about Beth's death. Unfortunately, the letter couldn't reach Amy in time for her to attend Beth's funeral. Besides, Aunt March was too ill to survive the sea voyage[1] with Amy anyway.

Amy did reply and confirm that she would arrange her return trip as soon as Aunt March got better, hopefully in time to celebrate Meg's baby with the family.

Check Up Choose the correct answer.

T F 1. Amy wanted to come home for Beth's funeral but Aunt March disallowed her to do so.

Ans: F

1. **voyage** [ˋvɔɪdʒ] (n.) 航行；旅行

After Beth's funeral, Jo found it difficult to crawl out of her tunnel of sorrow.

As the only daughter who lived at home, Jo was occupied with daily errands[2] while consoling[3] her parents. However, in her idle[4] moments, old memories crept into her mind wherever she looked.

There were Beth's working boots lying on the shelf in the hallway covered with dirt; that navy blue apron[5] Beth used to wear was still hung on the back of a chair in the kitchen. Jo felt it was too overwhelming for her to get over the loss of her beloved sister. She was afraid that she would suffer a mental handicap for the rest of her life.

"When will we ever be together again?" she sadly asked herself.

She then wrote a letter sealed with sorrow and joy to Laurie to inform him of Beth's death and Meg's pregnancy.

✓ Check Up Choose the correct answer.

T F 2. Jo felt that she might never get over the heartache of losing Beth.

Ans: T

2. **errand** [ˋɛrənd] (n.) 差事
3. **console** [kənˋsoʊl] (v.) 安慰
4. **idle** [ˋaɪdl] (a.) 空閒的；無所事事的
5. **apron** [ˋeɪprən] (n.) 圍裙

Usually Jo was kept so busy during the day that she didn't feel much of her pain and lonesomeness[1].

As the sun dipped below the horizon, Jo was stacking stuff away up in the attic[2].

She found an old bin[3] and remembered how Beth used to call it her treasure chest. Jo's fingers slowly reached for the wooden carved handle but hesitated to open it. After a few seconds, she boosted herself and let old memories take her away.

Inside the treasure chest were the deck of playing cards Amy had made, the bow and arrow Jo used to play with, and the pieces of floral[4] fabric from Meg's favorite old skirt.

Check Up Choose the correct answer.

T F 3. Jo found Beth's treasure chest in the basement, but she didn't open it.

Ans: F

1. **lonesomeness** [`lounsəmnɪs] (n.) 寂寞；孤單
2. **attic** [`ætɪk] (n.) 閣樓；頂樓房間
3. **bin** [bɪn] (n.) （儲藏物品用的）箱子
4. **floral** [`flɔːrəl] (a.) 花的

🎧 56

All these items Beth had preserved and cherished had long ago been either thrown away or abandoned by her sisters. There was also a stone tablet the sisters used to practice writing and drawing on, and a booklet[1] their mother made that recorded their birth dates, colors of their eyes and hair, and their weight when they were born.

One thing that especially pinched Jo's heart was their father's brass medal[2] that he gave Beth to award her for combating her illness when she was a little girl.

Jo couldn't help but chew over[3] each item stored in Beth's treasure chest and the stories behind them.

Check Up Choose the correct answer.

T F 4. The items stored in the treasure chest were no longer important to others but had been cherished by Beth.

Ans: T

1. **booklet** ['buklɪt] (n.) 小冊子
2. **medal** ['medl] (n.) 勳章；紀念章
3. **chew over** 深思；細想

· Chapter Eighteen ·

🎧57 Celebrating New Life Together

Jo's thoughts moved like atoms[1] that are pulled by invisible gravity[2], and suddenly all the loose pieces of a jigsaw[3] puzzle united in her mind. She dug out her portable typewriter and started writing a true story.

The heroines[4] in her biography were no other than herself and her sisters. Without sophisticated plotting, Jo simply rebuilt warm-hearted details from her memory of daily life. She wrote with the greatest pleasure, and eventually, her words would touch women around the world.

✓*Check Up* Choose the correct answer.

T F 5. After retrieving her old memories, Jo was so inspired that she finally wrote her own story.

Ans: T

1. **atom** [ˋætəm] (n.) 原子
2. **gravity** [ˋgrævəti] (n.)
   地心引力；重力
3. **jigsaw** [ˋdʒɪgsɔ:] (n.) 拼圖
4. **heroine** [ˋheroʊɪn] (n.)
   （故事中的）女主角

58

As the autumn chill breezed[1] through the suburbs of a city in mainland Europe, Laurie arrived at the lobby of a hotel with his trunk to meet Amy.

For the past months, he had worked very hard for his grandfather by helping regulate international commerce. He had helped to keep the company from going bankrupt and even to surpass[2] its rivals[3].

Laurie believed it would be a good time to propose to Amy, but his plan must have a brake as Aunt March was on her deathbed[4]. Aunt March passed away several days later without much suffering, and shortly after, Laurie and Amy embarked on their journey home.

 Check Up Choose the correct answer.

T F 1. Laurie and Amy wanted to make sure that Aunt March would have the right injection before they went home.

 Ans: F

1. **breeze** [briːz] (v.) 吹著微風
2. **surpass** [sɚˋpæs] (v.) 勝過
3. **rival** [ˋraɪvl] (n.) 對手;競爭者
4. **deathbed** [ˋdɛθbɛd] (n.) 臨終(所臥的床)

Back in Concord in the United States, the March family was nervously waiting at Meg and John's place.

"Congratulations!" the midwife[5] said to John as she opened the bedroom door where Meg had just successfully given birth.

"Is it a boy or a girl?" John asked hastily.

"Yes, both!" The midwife's misleading[6] answer confused John. She continued, "They are twins."

John instantly burst into a great laugh. His jaw almost fell out of his chin as he rushed into the room to see his wife and children.

"Little bundles of love. Welcome to the March family," Jo uttered as she held the newborns. "I am Auntie Jo. I can't wait to play with you. Let me be your friend. I will take you to explore the world." She then announced that she would be more than happy to share the grind[7] of cooking and washing for Meg, so she could devote all her attention to the babies.

Check Up Choose the correct answer.

T F 2. John and Meg became parents of both a boy and a girl.

Ans: T

5. **midwife** ['mɪdwaɪf] (n.) 助產士　7. **grind** [graɪnd] (n.) 苦差事
6. **misleading** [ˌmɪs'liːdɪŋ]
  (a.) 使人誤解的

59

Meanwhile, a carriage stopped at the Marches' house briefly and then arrived at John and Meg's place. It was Laurie and Amy; they were just in time to join this celebratory[1] moment. Mrs. March opened the front door to greet Laurie. He looked into the house and said, "Great! Everyone is here. I would like you to meet my wife." Then he stepped aside. To everyone's surprise, Laurie's wife, the young lady standing behind him, was Amy.

Laurie and Amy were first congratulated and then introduced to the newest members of the family, whom Mr. March had named Daisy and Demi.

"Well, Amy and I forecasted[2] the sex of the baby, and whoever loses the bet has to buy the other dessert. Now since we both lost, or won, we should treat everyone."

Check Up Choose the correct answer.

T F 3. When Laurie showed up at the Marches' house, no one knew that he and Amy were married.

T F 4. Laurie and Amy invited everyone for dinner to celebrate their wedding.

Ans: T, F

1. **celebratory** [`seləbrə‚tɔ:ri] (a.) 興高采烈的
2. **forecast** [`fɔ:rkæst] (v.) 預測

60

Laurie then ordered his servant to buy a dozen cups of puddings with toppings[1] of assorted nuts from his favorite bakery and also to bring his grandfather over for such an extraordinarily happy occasion.

Amy asked Jo if she minded that she got married with Laurie. "I am surprised since I never imagined your union," Jo replied. "I am really happy that the drift of pursuing your different goals brought you together while living abroad. But you must promise me one thing that you will always live close by the family. I couldn't bear losing another sister."

✓ *Check Up* Choose the correct answer.

T F 5. Jo hoped the newlyweds would not have to move too far away.

Ans: T

---

1. **topping** [ˈtɑːpɪŋ] (n.) 覆蓋在甜點上面的一層

The blissfully sweet taste of the pudding intensified[2] the gratifying experience as it melted on everyone's tongue. Jo considered it was a representative happy finale[3] for her story of common civilian life. It had been a while since the last time her folks gathered in such ecstasy. She was deeply moved and overall rejuvenated[4] by the energy of life that evolves from human ancestors to the newborn babies.

2. **intensify** [ɪnˋtensɪfaɪ] (v.)
   加強；增強
3. **finale** [fɪˋnæli] (n.) 終曲；末章
4. **rejuvenate** [rɪˋdʒuːvəneɪt]
   (v.) 使恢復精神

· Chapter Nineteen ·

61 A New Plan for an Old Mansion

For Jo, the writing process was like living alone in a cave. Only then could she comfortably create her own reality in words. From a comparative[1] viewpoint, one might say it was no different from being in jail, except writers do so willingly and produce works as the legacy[2] of humanity.

Jo had become proficient in capturing the primitive[3] state of emotions, which she believed was the cord of every aesthetic expression.

Whenever a flash of ideas popped out, she scratched it out on paper before integrating it into her story. Like a well-trained spy who observes tiny clues, Jo had beautifully woven all the substantive[4] pieces together.

Check Up Choose the correct answer.

T F 1. Jo liked to hang around and chat with people when she was writing so she could get her inspirations to accord with their conversation.
Ans: F

1. **comparative** [kəmˋpærətɪv] (a.) 比較的;相對的

2. **legacy** [ˋlegəsi] (n.) 遺產;留給後人的東西

Finally, Jo thoroughly checked to ensure consistency as she wrapped up her story, and then she daintily[5] signed across the seal on her manuscript and sent it to New York for Mr. Bhaer's comments.

Aunt March had no children, but she unexpectedly willed to Jo the inheritance of her mansion.

One day, Mrs. March and Jo went to inspect the property. Its convenient location was a plus, and it even included a stable[6], barn, and a dock for some boating or fishing in the nearby lake. Inside the mansion, the floors, windows, and furniture were covered with dust.

"I never noticed there are so many fireplaces! I wonder if the chimneys are all clogged[7]," Jo uttered astonishingly.

"You will need a handy[8] man and a gardener to fix some problems and plant some trees," Mrs. March suggested.

Check Up Choose the correct answer.

T F 2. Because of Aunt March's will, Jo received a nice piece of property.

Ans: T

3. **primitive** [ˈprɪmətɪv] (a.) 原始的
4. **substantive** [səbˈstæntɪv] (a.) 獨立的
5. **daintily** [ˈdeɪntɪli] (adv.) 優美地
6. **stable** [ˈsteɪbl] (n.) 馬廄
7. **clog** [klɑːg] (v.) 阻塞
8. **handy** [ˈhændi] (a.) 手巧的

62

"It's huge! What can I do with this place?" Jo asked.

"This is a perfect place to start a school," Mrs. March remarked.

Jo was in accord with[1] this proposal and excitingly consulted with her mother. As the executive director, Jo would need special approval from the mayor and the education bureau[2] to offer courses for civilians.

Since the March family had long been involved in community service, Jo wanted to expand her program to help poor children to receive better education.

Her management would be classified as a non-profit organization, which also qualified for sanctions such as donations to the school being deductible[3] on income tax.

✓ *Check Up* Choose the correct answer.

T F 3. Mrs. March suggested Jo open an aquarium to preserve wild life.

Ans: F

---

1. **in accord with** 同⋯⋯一致
2. **bureau** [ˋbjʊroʊ] (n.) （政府機構）署；處；局；司
3. **deductible** [dɪˋdʌktəbl] (a.) 可扣除的

63

Jo still needed more money in order to run a school. She wanted to invite professional performers as the cast to perform in the stadium[1] to raise funds. Mrs. March would recruit[2] and manage volunteers from acquaintances and nuns of local churches.

Since there was a recent boom of tourism, Mrs. March made a forecast that this event would steer a great deal of public attention toward long-term support.

After a stimulating discussion, Jo arrived home and found someone had delivered a package to her and left.

She quickly opened it and realized that it was her story, along with a letter from a publisher and a contract proposal. Jo questioned herself who might have delivered the package to her, and she could think of only one person, Mr. Bhaer.

Check Up Choose the correct answer.

T F 4. Jo planned to raise money through hosting a performance, but Mrs. March was afraid that the government would tax their profits.

T F 5. Jo guessed that Mr. Bhaer had delivered the package to her.

Ans: F, T

1. **stadium** [ˈsteɪdɪəm] (n.) 體育館
2. **recruit** [rɪˈkruːt] (v.) 徵募（新兵）；招收（新成員）

· Chapter Twenty ·

🎧 64 Settling in Love

Jo yearned to find out and asked, "Hannah! Do you know who delivered this package?"

"A middle-aged man with a strange last name and a foreign accent showed up with that package half an hour ago. I thought he was Amy and Laurie's friend, the European ambassador[1], coming to deliver a wedding gift. So I told him that since Ms. March got married to Mr. Laurence, they have now moved to the house next door. Then he said he had a train to catch and left."

✓ Check Up Choose the correct answer.

_____ 1. According to Hannah, a strange man showed up half an hour ago with _____.
    Ⓐ an aluminum rod
    Ⓑ a spray of perfume
    Ⓒ a bundle of papers

Ans: C

"Oh, no!" Jo roared as she hastily ran like a bullet toward the train station.

Her heart was bouncing in suspension[2], and her mind was totally blank[3].

The train station was very crowded when Jo got in. She glanced over every face but couldn't recognize anyone. Finally, a man who was helping an elderly woman standing in front of him to get on a cart caught her attention. "Mr. Bhaer!" Jo yelled with full force.

He looked around to identify the source of the voice, but the upward movement of other passengers trying to get on the train obscured[4] it. Jo kept yelling and stepped onto a stool until Mr. Bhaer saw her.

Check Up Choose the correct answer.

_____ 2. Jo noticed Mr. Bhaer when he was helping an old lady to _____.
Ⓐ screw the lid off of a jar
Ⓑ step on the train
Ⓒ recognize the voice from a tape recorder

Ans: B

1. **ambassador** [æm`bæsədər] (n.) 大使
2. **suspension** [sə`spenʃən] (n.) 懸掛；懸浮
3. **blank** [blæŋk] (a.) 空白的
4. **obscure** [əb`skjur] (v.) 遮蓋

◯ 65

After swimming through the crowd, they finally reached each other.

"Reading your book was like opening a window into your heart. I am so proud and happy to see that you have beautifully blossomed and embraced your true self," Mr. Bhaer praised.

"Do you have to get back to New York so soon?" Jo asked.

"Actually I just decided to move to the West Coast. I heard there is more demand for professors there. My friend said that I could start as a substitute for the intermediate[1] Germen course at any time," Mr. Bhaer reluctantly[2] expressed.

Check Up Choose the correct answer.

T F 3. The motive for Mr. Bhaer to relocate to the West Coast was to have a better chance of becoming a teacher.

Ans: T

1. **intermediate** [ˌɪntərˈmiːdiət] (a.) 中級的；中等程度的
2. **reluctantly** [rɪˈlʌktəntli] (adv.) 不情願地

Jo told Mr. Bhaer about her project of setting up a school and asked him, "Would you consider working with me? I think you are the best candidate to be the headmaster³ of my school."

After a confusing silence, he uttered awkwardly, "Thank you for your offer, but I don't want to disturb your marriage."

Jo immediately straightened up by saying, "Oh, no! That was my younger sister Amy who married Laurie."

Check Up Choose the correct answer.

T F 4. The reason Mr. Bhaer initially rejected Jo's offer was because he thought Jo and Laurie were married.

Ans: T

3. **headmaster** [ˋhedˌmæstər] (n.) 私立學校校長

They had a good laugh for such a comedy-like mistake. Then Jo continued, "I hope you can stay here with me and be my guardian[1] for my professional and personal life." Jo's sincere words instantly lit up[2] Mr. Bhaer's face as he fell into a state of bliss[3].

As our story approaches to the end, the March family was having an incredible harvest. The school founded by Jo and Mr. Bhaer was credited as the best private educational institution after surveying[4] the opinions of the students and the parents in the county.

Jo's story was published and became a huge success nation-wide. She was recognized as the most influential female writer among her contemporaries[5]. Having been through all the hardships, the March family could finally reap[6] the fruits of prosperity, with their dreams fulfilled and legends to pass on.

Check Up Choose the correct answer.

T F 5. Jo was successful as the founder of her school and a financial analyst.

Ans: F

1. **guardian** [`gɑːrdiən] (n.) 守護者
2. **lit up** 照亮
3. **bliss** [blɪs] (n.) 極樂；至喜
4. **survey** [sɜːr`veɪ] (v.) 調查
5. **contemporary** [kən`tempəreri] (n.) 同時代的人
6. **reap** [riːp] (v.) 收穫；獲得

Exercises

A Multiple Choice.

_____ ❶ How did Meg meet her future husband?
   (a) A matchmaker arranged a blind date for her.
   (b) She met him at the annual republican convention.
   (c) He is a senior in her school who later works for her father.
   (d) He used to be the tutor of her neighbor.

_____ ❷ According to Jo, what did John steal from Meg?
   (a) Her handkerchief.
   (b) Her digital camera.
   (c) Her glove.
   (d) Her rifle.

_____ ❸ What did Jo do to support her family when they were in need?
   (a) She cut her long hair and sold it when faced with financial emergency.
   (b) She opened the tap and filled up the tub with hot water.
   (c) She used solar power to operate a fridge.
   (d) She decided to move to New York to live with Mr. Bhaer.

_____ ④ Which of the following does not belong to Beth's daily routine?

(a) Sharing food with the poor neighbors.
(b) Wearing her overall to do the laundry and cooking at home.
(c) Going to the church to do cleaning for the monks.
(d) Collecting memorable items for her family.

_____ ⑤ Why did Hannah suggest sending Amy away when Beth had scarlet fever?

(a) She was afraid the mineral and vitamin in the drinking water wasn't enough.
(b) Since Laurie wanted to take Amy on the ferry to visit Aunt March.
(c) So Amy wouldn't catch this infectious disease from Beth.
(d) To substitute for Jo who was sentenced to life in prison.

_____ ⑥ Which of the following Mrs. March's statements is true?

(a) I hope my girls will bear the hatred of money.
(b) Tons of happiness can be harbored in a humble cabin.
(c) Cultivating a well of joy is less worthwhile than having money.
(d) Social status and money can only be interference for love and virtue.

_____ ❼ Which of the following statements can best describe Meg's ideal wedding?

(a) Her preferred location is the Emperor's garden.
(b) She wishes to dress up like a totally different person and wear a helmet.
(c) She would be happy to see the wedding to be halted by someone she loves.
(d) She doesn't want an extravagant wedding.

_____ ❽ How could Amy afford to study abroad?

(a) Someone spent a great fortune bidding all her paintings at the auctions.
(b) Her aunt who later became a terminal patient sponsored her.
(c) She was awarded a scholarship by an educational foundation.
(d) She divorced a rich man and got tons of money.

_____ ❾ How did Mrs. March react to Jo's request to leave home?

(a) She tensed up after knowing Jo's request.
(b) She agreed and assisted her with proper arrangement.
(c) She blamed it for her thinking patterns and ignored her.
(d) She disagreed with her but still let her go.

_____ ⑩ Which of the following statements about Jo was correct?

(a) She moved to Europe and was accused of being a murderer.
(b) She changed her career and became a surgeon.
(c) She was the underground leader of her tribe.
(d) She established a private school with the inheritance.

_____ ⑪ Which of the following statements about Amy was correct?

(a) She is recognized as a young and gifted artist.
(b) She is the mistress of a well-known entertainer.
(c) She never has peaceful chats with her aunt.
(d) She is dull and defensive.

_____ ⑫ Which of the following occupations did Amy pursue because of her talent?

(a) A rider who jumps over flaming loops on the horseback.
(b) A proofreader who inspects the errors in the manuals.
(c) A devil that always stabs people in the back.
(d) An artist who became mastered in skills through repetition.

_____ ⑬ Which occupation did Laurie take on to assist his family business?

(a) A hostage hidden away in a barrel located in Europe.

(b) A trader specializes in international commerce.

(c) A politician dictates morning reports to his secretary to type down.

(d) A jet pilot who invades other nations for gaining natural resources.

_____ ⑭ Which of the following events consequently determines Laurie and Amy's relationship?

(a) Jo turned down Laurie's proposal and moved to New York.

(b) Laurie visited Amy when she was in Europe.

(c) Laurie blew horn at Amy when he saw her on the street.

(d) Amy gave the secret code to Laurie when she lived in Europe.

_____ ⑮ Which of the following is Jo's first impression of New York?

(a) There are many similarities between her hometown Concord and New York.

(b) She found people of all nationalities arrived to New York.

(c) There are many drains on the streets in New York.

(d) There is nothing stranger than the putting light bulbs all over the Statue of Liberty.

_____ ⑯ Which of the following occupations Jo has never involved?

    (a) Tutor.

    (b) Companion.

    (c) Writer.

    (d) Runner.

_____ ⑰ Under which of the following situation, Jo first noticed Mr. Bhaer?

    (a) She was fixing the hooks on the wall in Mrs. Kirke's café.

    (b) She saw him helping an elder move heavy stuff in the kitchen.

    (c) Mrs. Kirke taught her how trifles show character.

    (d) Her elbow touched his when they had breakfast sitting together one morning.

_____ ⑱ Which of the following statements is true about Mr. Bhaer?

    (a) He experimented on a particular breed of bear in German.

    (b) He calculated the casualties after a submarine crashed into a tourist cruise ship.

    (c) He had not published any books yet when he met Jo.

    (d) He was generous, well educated and could speak German fluently.

_____ ⑲ Which of the following is not one of Beth's final words?

(a) Take care of the parents for me.
(b) I am not afraid of death anymore, so let me commit suicide.
(c) Remember my love will always be with you.
(d) Love is the only thing that we can carry with us to the grave.

_____ ⑳ Which of the following descriptions is true according to the story?

(a) Amy's ambition is to decrease racial difference in the world.
(b) Beth recovered totally from the fever after receiving medical treatment.
(c) Jo wrote a story based on her own life and it was a big success.
(d) Few years after Meg and John got married, they greeted their first and only child.

B Complete the following excerpts using the correct form of the words provided.

(1)

satisfy	mention	offend	assume
admiration	invention	inheritance	assemble
rage	inspiration		

1. John's _____ for Meg was quite obvious on their first date.

2. When Jo found out that Amy had burnt her manually written script, she was drowned in _____.

3. Jo wished that modern medical _____ could save her sister's life.

4. After Beth gradually recovered from her fever, her family and friends _____ at the Marches' house to surprise her with Christmas gifts.

5. After Jo rejected Laurie's proposal, she wanted to make a change since her life style at home couldn't _____ her anymore.

6. Jo shared her writing with Mr. Bhaer for his critiques, but was _____ by his straightforwardness.

7. Jo found the _____ in Beth's treasure chest to start her own story.

8. Before Aunt March passed away, she willed to Jo the _____ of her mansion.

9. Without _____ to anyone, Laurie and Amy surprisingly showed up together at John and Meg's house.

10. Since Laurie and Amy just returned from Europe, Hannah _____ that Mr. Bhaer is their friend because of his European accent.

(2)

necessity	economic	comedy	remain
scarce	regularly	element	solution
neglect	invention		

1. It is a _____ to have electric sockets in the room to charge mobile phones and other electronics.

2. The current _____ boom has sucked many workers from abroad, especially the neighboring countries.

3. The only way to get to the pristine island is to take a ferry, which runs _____ throughout the summer.

4. The _____ was shot in a disco in town, where used to be the most happening spot during the 1970s.

5. These balloons can fly because they are filled up with hydrogen, the lightest and most abundant _____ in the universe.

6. This biodegradable _____ can kill all the unwanted worms and bacteria in the water or soil.

7. The parking in the urbane center is _____ and usually costly.

8. Extremely precise cutting on all kinds of materials can now be done because of the _____ of laser.

9. The global warming issue is too important to be _____, but we often occupied by other more urgent disasters.

10. The seasonal swimming of the salmon from the ocean to its origin in the river _____ a mystery.

C Discussion: Reading Comprehension.

1. Please specify when and where the story takes place with at least three indications from the story.

2. Please identify two incidents from the story to illustrate the hardships that the March family has been through.

3. Which character of the March sisters deserves the most pity and why?

4. What happened between Laurie and Jo that changed their relationship forever?

5. Please refer two incidents from the story after Jo moved to New York to show the extreme happy and sorrow turns toward the ending.

　　《小婦人》（*Little Women*）的作者露意莎・梅・奧爾柯特（Louisa May Alcott, 1832–1888）與三個姊妹生於美國麻薩諸塞州的首府：海港城市波士頓。

　　露意莎 8 歲時舉家遷至附近的康科特（Concord），雖然生活經常受貧窮所苦，但在這裡她度過最快樂的一段童年。奧爾柯特一家僅有一間樸質的小屋，但幾個女孩會在鄰近的穀倉表演露意莎寫的劇本。

　　露意莎在家自學，之後在波士頓當學校老師。20 歲時，她賣出第一篇作品，兩年後出版了第一本完整小說。越發成名後，書本的收入帶給家人較舒適的生活，減輕家庭負擔，這也是露意莎從寫作上獲得的最大滿足。《小婦人》1869 年出版，已成為美國經典文學之一。

　　《小婦人》描述馬區一家總是辛勤工作、勇於面對磨難的生活。雖然父親加入聯邦軍隊在外征戰，梅格、喬、貝絲與艾美四個姊妹與母親仍對生活保持樂觀。馬區太太在當地從事慈善事務，受她的影響，女孩們也總是慷慨幫助需要的人。

　　在聖誕季的一場盛大派對上，馬區家的姊妹遇見名為羅利的青年，並共度快樂時光。但因為父親受傷，女孩們必須面對真正的挑戰，也就是學會成長獨立。而在貝絲感染猩紅熱受病痛糾纏後，情況變得更加艱鉅。

　　經歷與愛人的分離重逢，以及追逐理想的向外冒險，馬區家的姊妹變得成熟，習得智慧，並從家庭生活中尋得幸福的真諦。

Mr. and Mrs. March 馬區先生與馬區太太

是四個可愛女兒的父母。美國南北戰爭（Civil War）期間，馬區先生效力於北方聯邦軍隊，馬區太太便負責照顧家庭。

Meg 梅格

最年長的女兒。個性貼心善解人意，為家庭犧牲奉獻。

Jo 喬

二女兒。個性坦率直言，十分沈浸於寫作的樂趣中。

Beth 貝絲

三女兒。個性安靜溫柔，喜歡彈奏鋼琴。

Amy 艾美

最小的女兒。有些調皮但十分可愛，對繪畫具有天分。

Aunt March 馬區嬸婆

馬區先生的嬸嬸，十分富有但生活孤單。

Laurie 羅利

馬區一家的鄰居，與祖父羅倫斯先生同居。羅利是富裕家庭裡的獨子，為人善良細心。

John 約翰

羅利的家庭教師，與梅格相愛。

[第一章] 馬區家的聖誕節

`p. 13` 萬物都覆上了白雪。對馬區家的女孩們來說,聖誕節又來臨了。她們渴望收到精緻的禮物,但是家中的經濟狀況卻拮据得什麼也買不起。

四個姐妹中最年長的梅格,開口嘆了口氣說:「沒有禮物實在不像聖誕節。」

最年幼的妹妹艾美,皺起眉頭,喃喃自語:「我真想要彩色鉛筆。」

二姊喬說:「說實話,要是不必為馬區嬸婆工作就好了,那個吝嗇的老太婆。」

貝絲則揚起眉毛說:「我只願戰爭結束,這樣爸爸就能回家……」

`p. 14` 「噢,好貝絲,妳說出了我們的心聲啊!」其他三個姐妹異口同聲地說道。

接著喬抒發了有朝一日成為作家的心願。艾美則對未來穿金戴銀充滿信心,因為她打定主意要嫁給有錢人。

艾美那句充滿哲理的話,更逗笑了姐姐們:「有一天我們都會長大,也會知道自己要的是什麼。」

當馬區太太一進門,女孩們就開心地喚著「媽媽」,衝向門邊迎接她。馬區太太帶回父親的信,讓女孩們十分驚喜,於是她們一起大聲讀信。

`p. 16` 知道父親平安健康,女孩們感到寬心。但一想到父親必須忍受與家人分隔兩地的寂寞,她們又感到失落。

感傷的思緒及時被節日的歡愉取代;女孩們唱著聖誕禮讚直到就寢。喬照常熬夜,用筆編織著她幻想中的世界。

聖誕節當天,梅格與女傭漢娜一同準備早餐,誘人的香氣喚醒了沈睡中的喬。馬區太太則已經出門,到一個叫作惠梅爾的德國家庭幫忙。

p. 17　　自從惠梅爾先生過世後,惠梅爾太太跟六個孩子就過著一貧如洗的生活。個性最為善良的貝絲,便說動姐妹們分送一些食物到惠梅爾家。

　　送完食物的回家途中,馬區姐妹注意到一個年輕人,正和他的祖父一起搬進附近一棟優雅的豪宅。

　　這位老人是羅倫斯先生,而年輕人則看來落落寡歡。出於好奇心,姐妹們整晚都在討論他的背景。

p. 18　　喬和梅格準備參加新年派對。

　　梅格為了派對盛裝打扮。喬一邊和其他姐妹聊天,一邊用熱鐵棒替梅格燙頭髮。貝絲則對於不必周旋在陌生人中間,可以在家與艾美作伴感到快活。

　　突然一陣焦味傳來,喬才發現梅格的頭髮已經毀在她手上了。這個意外引發了一陣慌亂,直到艾美在梅格燙壞的頭髮上綁了一個緞帶作裝飾,讓梅格恢復往常的美麗。

　　派對上,向梅格邀舞的年輕人很多,梅格一支接一支地跳著。喬則不經意地與新搬來的鄰居羅倫斯先生的孫子羅利巧遇,玩得十分盡興。

　　不料,梅格扭傷了腳踝,不得不提早離開。馬區家的新朋友羅利,好心地用馬車送馬區姐妹一程,讓她們舒服地到家,她們因此感激在心。

[第二章] 每天的例行工作

p. 20 聖誕假期結束了，女孩們還是得天天早起，從早忙到晚。

一天早晨，當梅格站在門外等待妹妹們，羅利和他的家庭教師——個叫做約翰·布魯克的年輕人正好路過。在女孩們開始一天的奔波之前，他們簡單地打了招呼。

馬區姐妹們很早就開始接觸外面的世界，唯獨貝絲除外。她太害羞，連學校也不敢去。儘管她曾試著去上學，但害羞的個性卻讓她非常不自在。

她先在家跟著父親讀書，甚至當父母都忙時，她便自己往下讀，能讀多少算多少。她也幫忙漢娜煮飯和整理家務。

p. 21 「噢，親愛的妹妹，我真提不起勁回托兒所工作。」梅格嘆道。

「我希望永遠都放假。」喬鬱悶地打了個哈欠答道。陪伴馬區嬸婆這份工作對她來說也很沒意思。這位膝下無子的老太太行動不便，需要有個行動自如的人隨侍在側。

艾美緊接著兩個姐姐說：「我想做貝絲，這樣就能待在家，專做有意義的消遣。」

p. 22 「可不是，如果妳把家務事看作一種有意義的消遣！」喬說。

喬的評語澆了艾美一頭冷水。「那羅利呢？他有上學嗎？」艾美問。

「他請了家庭教師，記得吧？就是我們剛才碰到的那個人，我忘了他叫什麼來著。」喬說。

「布魯克先生，他還說我們可以叫他約翰。」梅格想起來了。

「對，我覺得……」喬的話被艾美幾近哀號的叫聲打斷。

「今天我得帶東西去學校請客。同學總是請我，我欠他們太多了……」

由於艾美不斷哀求，梅格終於給了她一個 25 分硬幣，讓她買點東西請同學吃。

p. 24　艾美有著傑出的繪畫天分。她的老師抱怨她的筆記本上總是滿滿的圖畫，而不是算好的數學作業。

艾美盡量維持水準以上的學習成績。學校裡，大家都知道她脾氣好，又擁有藝術才能。

稍晚，艾美哭著回家。她的雙手腫了起來。她用從梅格那裡求來的錢，精打細算買了點東西，卻不肯分點好處給同學，於是引發了一陣騷動。她頂撞老師，受到了處罰。

p. 26　馬區太太寫了一封信向學校表達她的失望，並且決定讓艾美待在家裡由喬來教她。馬區太太甚至提到，如果喬找不到合適的教材，她可以請羅利的家庭教師布魯克先生幫忙。

雖然喬絲毫不想監督艾美的課業，卻找不到任何藉口拒絕母親，她只好不情願地答應母親接下了這件差事。

梅格是艾美的密友，也是她的督導。熱情的喬和害羞的貝絲性格南轅北轍，卻難以解釋地互相吸引而非常要好。

兩個較年長的姐姐，梅格和喬，彼此親密為伴，卻又各自以自己的方式教導其中另外一個妹妹。正如人們所說的「扮演母職」，自然流露出小婦人的母性本能。

[第三章] 艾美的報復和喬的盛怒

p. 28 馬區家的女孩經常以排演喬寫的劇本作為消遣。近來羅利好幾次加入排演，這一晚還計劃帶喬和梅格一同外出看戲。

艾美抱怨著說：「我想去劇院。我每次哪裡都不能去。」

當她準備好了，喬卻回答道：「妳還太小。」

艾美很沮喪，爭辯道：「我不小了。妳只想獨占羅利。我可以去嗎，拜託？」

「艾美，我想羅利只拿到四張票。」梅格解釋道。

喬繼續說：「不要鬧了。只有梅格、我、羅利，和那個悶葫蘆布魯克先生。」

p. 29 艾美哀求喬問羅利能不能再拿到一張票，但喬拒絕了。貝絲提議為艾美煮些薑茶，並說艾美既然感冒了，就應該待在家裡休息。

離開前，喬規定艾美練習好幾頁數學習題。喬在家教導艾美很嚴格，常常指正、批評她懶散的地方。

姐姐們走後，艾美極度不開心。她一向天真無邪，當下心中卻被一股惡作劇的念頭所占據。

p. 30 幾個小時後，約翰和梅格在回家路上，興致勃勃地大談彼此對於戲劇的熱愛。羅利和喬跟在後面，發現他們之間起了火花；至少約翰對梅格的愛慕是顯而易見的。

基於保護立場，喬一點也不願接受將姐姐與約翰配成一對，於是她莽撞地打斷他們，推著梅格回家。

當她們進門時，馬區太太還醒著，正在客廳工作。梅格和喬向她簡短地報告了看戲的心得。

喬記掛著要寫些東西，便先離開回到自己的房間。喬看到艾美在讀書，便問艾美心情有沒有好一點，不過艾美什麼也沒回答。

p.31 臥房裡，貝絲已經睡著了。喬找不到她的稿子，因此猜想可能是貝絲拿去讀又忘了放回去。當喬瞥見房裡的壁爐，卻震驚地看到她的稿子在火裡燒著。

喬的尖叫聲可能幾哩外都聽得見，但是來不及了，爐火燒毀了所有的作品。艾美為了報復喬而燒了她的稿子。

喬怒氣沖天，把艾美拖下床，生氣地揮舞著拳頭質問她。艾美簡直嚇呆了，全身發抖。對喬的指控她無法辯解，只能默認。

p.32 「我恨妳，永遠不會原諒妳。」喬哭著一邊反覆低聲地重複這幾個字。她崩潰了，但是她的拳頭並沒有打在艾美身上，而只是用力捶著地板。

馬區太太和梅格聽到吵鬧聲便立刻趕過去，發現事情糟得無法想像。情況太複雜了，一時之間無法輕易解決。

梅格把艾美帶到一旁，讓馬區太太安慰喬。馬區太太希望喬和艾美很快能恢復往日的和諧。

[第四章] 女人的責任與美麗

p.34 從那晚的衝突過後，喬就再也沒和艾美說話。一天，喬和羅利冒險到結凍的湖上溜冰，艾美一路跟著他們，即使喬始終看也不看她。

湖面上有幾處因為冰太薄而裂開了。艾美掉進冰水中，大喊救命。幸虧喬和羅利離得不遠，救了艾美，讓她撿回一命。

這件事終於為喬和艾美的冷戰劃上句點，兩人和好如初。

p. 35 春天，梅格準備參加一個派對，馬區姐妹忙著替她張羅身上的行頭。這種社交場合總能讓年輕人如願遇到好對象。

媒婆拜訪了馬區家，提醒他們也差不多是時間替梅格找個合適的好對象了。媒婆提醒馬區太太，梅格的婚姻也許有助於解決馬區家的經濟困境。

就在出門前，梅格找不到她的派對手套，只好借用馬區太太的。她忍不住想著，要是能有多一副手套該有多好，而或許嫁個有錢人會是個好主意。

p. 36 梅格一踏進派對，便無法抗拒奢侈的欲望，想穿上有錢女孩的備用晚禮服並濃妝豔抹一番。她像隻花蝴蝶一樣四處周旋，展露自己的魅力，內心陶醉不已。

同時，羅利也在派對中，並且將梅格虛榮的一面完全看在眼裡。他私下調侃梅格的虛假。梅格對自己膚淺的行為感到羞恥，請求羅利不要讓妹妹們知道自己在派對上的模樣。諷刺地是，他們的對話卻招來旁觀者的竊竊私語。

p. 38 回家後，梅格和喬在馬區太太面前討論，社會對待男女兩性的標準是如何不同。梅格質疑為什麼女人總是成為批評的對象，特別要是她享受與男人眉目傳情，但一模一樣的行為卻無損男人的名譽。馬區太太對於世界上的雙重標準感到遺憾。

「確實，男人總是比女人擁有較為優越的地位。男人能投票，掌握財富，從事任何喜愛的職業。」馬區太太說。

「然而，女人卻被禁止做這些事。彷彿對我們女人來說，成為家庭主婦是唯一出路，活著就是為了生兒育女。」喬不滿地說。

p. 39　喬覺得男女地位不平等是很荒謬的事。她認為女人應該順從個人意志，不在乎他人的看法，絕不隨波逐流。梅格不同意，因為她在意別人的眼光，她喜歡打扮得漂漂亮亮，並接受讚美和寵愛。

　　馬區太太告訴梅格，自己怎麼看待自己，要比其他人的想法重要多了。如果她認為自己的價值只像一種裝飾，那就大大限制了個人的潛能。

　　「時間會抹去所有表面的美，而女人擁有的智慧和道德勇氣，才能真正恆久不變。男人與女人都應該將這種品格放在第一位。」馬區太太總結道。

[第五章] 鬱鬱寡歡的喬和不幸的消息

p. 40　近來，喬悶悶不樂，情緒低落，因為羅利將要在新學期前往哈佛唸書。照羅利的時間表，他得開始收拾行李了。

　　在喬的陪伴和幫忙下，羅利在祖父的房子裡打包東西。喬不斷把成疊的書遞給羅利，讓他帶在身上；那都是他們曾經一起讀過的。

　　羅利委婉地對喬說：「我覺得那些書不需要帶，畢竟我沒有時間再讀一次。」

p. 42　「當然你不會有時間。你會有更重要的東西要念，因為你將成為高知識分子了。你的同學們都是像你一樣的好學生，鑽研更高深的學問，最後畢業後將成為學者。不像我，未來沒有定數，只能成為某個領域的業餘工作者。」喬這樣挖苦自己。

　　她感覺糟透了，彷彿將要被最好的朋友遺棄。她接著說：「我看你的未來再也容不下那些書了。」

羅利反駁道：「喬，一切都還是一樣。我們還是最好的朋友，就算我們未來走的路不同。再說，我覺得我的路並沒有妳的明確，因為我不像妳總是對未來充滿雄心壯志。」

p. 43　喬的眼神飄忽，失去往常的明亮堅定。她毫無生氣地說：「你會在新環境中碰到各種美好的遭遇、新奇的體驗，當你回來的時候，你知道的事情多了，懂得的道理也多了，我們之間就會變得無話可說。」

　　「雖然妳這樣說有點誇張，但我不得不說有件事是我知道而妳卻毫無所覺的，就是……關於梅格和我的前任家庭教師，約翰・布魯克先生的事。」羅利試著轉移喬的注意力來哄她。

　　喬挑起眉毛，用懷疑的眼神質問羅利：「你在說什麼？他們偷偷在交往？我不相信你說的。」

　　羅利回答：「梅格不是弄丟了一只手套嗎？我知道約翰珍藏著那只手套，而且隨身放在他的口袋裡。」

p. 44　事情似乎有蹊蹺，喬趕忙回家告訴梅格，或許更確切地說，跟她對質。「約翰等於是偷了妳的私人物品，妳不覺得受到冒犯了嗎？」

　　梅格漲紅了臉卻不回答。

　　之後喬繼續說：「結果根本不是手套消失這樣奇怪的事，原來是約翰偷了妳的手套。」

　　梅格這才答道：「約翰實在不像是會做那種事的人。我覺得他很成熟，是個正直的人。他一定是在無意中撿到我的手套，卻沒有機會還給我。」

　　喬立即說：「妳現在開始護著他了……」

p. 45　此時，馬區太太衝進餐廳打斷了兩姐妹的談話。她的聲音抖著，彷彿隨時要昏倒。「喬、梅格！我剛收到電報……從華盛頓醫院來的，妳們父親受傷了。」

這個不幸的消息讓馬區家的一切都失控了，所有人隨即陷入極度的緊張和焦慮中。

[第六章] 馬區太太的遠行

p. 46 馬區太太決定盡快去看馬區先生。然而，馬區家沒有多餘的錢能夠支付火車票。由於馬區太太已將珠寶全數賣掉，她便讓喬到馬區嬸婆家借些錢。

同時，其他姐妹則為馬區太太準備一些行李。貝絲為馬區太太摺衣服，艾美要馬區太太帶著毯子以防夜裡太涼。

p. 47 儘管馬區太太覺得女兒們都大得可以照顧自己，她還是給她們分配了不同的任務。她先指派梅格記帳，又要求貝絲確認惠梅爾家有足夠的食物和柴火，還要小艾美答應會乖乖聽話。

此時剛好羅利和約翰也來馬區家探望。羅利說：「馬區先生受傷實在是件不幸的事情。祖父包的這些火腿片和鑲甜椒，可以在路上吃。」

「謝謝。」馬區太太感激地說。

接著，梅格將約翰介紹給母親。

p. 48 約翰很有禮貌且誠懇地解釋：「因為羅利不再需要家庭教師了，羅倫斯先生便替我在華盛頓安排了一個工作。由於戰爭的緣故，現在旅行的風險更高了，就怕在途中遇到搶劫。我很願意護送您，請讓我將您安全送達目的地。希望您不要介意我已經預訂了下班列車的座位，傍晚六點出發。」

馬區太太感動不已，因為她非常清楚一個女人單獨旅行有多危險。她感激地說：「布魯克先生，您太好心了。」

「我們該動身去火車站了吧？」約翰問。

「是的，但我還想等一等喬。」馬區太太擔心地說。

p. 49 「喬為什麼這麼慢？」艾美問。

「為了錢跟馬區嬸婆打交道不容易。」梅格回答道。

突然，喬穿著連帽斗篷從前門進來了。跑得筋疲力竭的喬，將 25 元交到母親手裡時，還上氣不接下氣的。

馬區太太一看，不敢相信地說：「馬區嬸婆很少這麼大方。」

「這不是馬區嬸婆的錢。我為我那無用的長髮找到了正當的用途。」喬把帽子拿下回道。

所有的人都大吃一驚，喬美麗的長髮不見了。

「天哪！」馬區太太大叫。

「我不願踐踏尊嚴，浪費時間求馬區嬸婆借錢給我們，所以我賣了自己的頭髮。」喬若無其事地說。

p. 50 艾美吐吐舌頭，「妳哪來的勇氣！頭髮是妳全身上下唯一稱得上美的東西……」

梅格阻止艾美再說下去，並接著問：「為什麼不把銅水壺賣了？」

「不行。我們需要燒開水。只是頭髮而已，沒什麼大不了的，還會再長出來的不是嗎？必要的時候，我還是有辦法讓自己看來優雅的。」喬用開玩笑的方式將嚴肅的話題弄得輕鬆點。

馬區太太完全沉浸在感恩中，情緒一來，終於忍不住哭了。擁有這幾個了不起的女兒，讓她感到很幸運。

她抱了喬，親了她的額頭說：「我的寶貝女兒，非常謝謝妳的犧牲。」

馬區全家擁抱在一起，流下了會心的眼淚，輕聲呢喃著：「上帝保佑我們。」

[第七章] 馬區家的困境與貝絲的病

p. 52 在馬區姐妹準備早餐時，梅格告訴妹妹們一個消息。當梅格去牛奶舖取一品脫的牛奶時，店家要求她把賒的帳款付清，否則就不能再拿牛奶了。

事實上，自從父親因為戰爭離家後，她們就深陷在債務麻煩中。

艾美把烤盤從烤箱中取出來的時候，有兩塊餅乾掉了出來。「喔，可惡！我搞砸了。」艾美叫道。

「沒關係，我們還是會吃的。」她的姐姐們回答道。

p. 53 喬意外地發現桌上出現一些香腸。她立刻嚐了一塊，卻露出怪異的表情，問道：「這是什麼怪味？」

「那是豬肝做的。我們沒有多餘的預算，只買得起這種肉。」梅格回答道。

艾美建議：「也許我們可以都吃素。至少我只要有小麥麵包就可以活了。」

總是充滿愛心、樂善好施的貝絲問：「今天我可以帶什麼去惠梅爾家？」

梅格微笑著說：「先填飽妳的肚子吧。我會額外烤幾個馬鈴薯給他們。」

儘管馬區姐妹經濟狀況拮据，不過她們仍然樂於幫助窮人。

p. 54 早餐後，貝絲帶著馬鈴薯，跟平常一樣來到惠梅爾家的小屋。惠梅爾家是新移民，不會說英語，因此貝絲不懂惠梅爾太太想表達的話。

惠梅爾太太把懷中哭泣的嬰兒推向她，示意貝絲抱住嬰兒。

貝絲出於直覺反應，將嬰兒一把抱起，接著她才明白嬰兒正發著異常的高燒。貝絲非常同情可憐的惠梅爾家。

喬下班後立刻回家,因為羅利從學校放假回來了。她從信箱中取出一週的信件,在門廊前作分類,並驚訝地發現有封她的信。

p. 55 她急切地想要讀信,當場把信撕開,沒多久就大叫著跑進屋子。「我賣出了我的第一個故事!五塊錢!我是作家了!」

她覺得自己為家庭的經濟狀況找到了一個穩固的解決之道。但屋內沒有人答腔。

「大概沒人在家,」喬想。接著她走進客廳,看到貝絲躺在躺椅上,蓋著羊毛毯。

「怎麼了?」喬問。

貝絲說不出話來,只是眨了眨眼。喬摸了摸她的額頭,發現她是因為高燒才會這麼虛弱。

因為馬區太太離家在外,姐妹們不知道該拿貝絲的病怎麼辦。她們只知道貝絲的病一定是受惠梅爾家的嬰兒傳染的。於是梅格耐心地把馬區太太的醫書從頭到尾翻過一遍。

p. 56 一會兒,家裡的女傭漢娜從惠梅爾家回來了。她汗流浹背、氣喘吁吁地說:「上帝已經帶走了兩個孩子,都是惠梅爾家的!有些鄰居說那是猩紅熱。」

她繼續對喬和梅格說:「妳們兩個比較大的不會有事,因為妳們小時候都得過了。」

接著,她轉向艾美,態度堅決地說:「但是艾美,我們得把妳送走。這種傳染病足以致命,這是唯一一個保護妳的方法。」

p. 58 稍晚，羅利用馬車把艾美送到馬區嬸婆家。

艾美感到悲傷，絕望地哭著說：「真是太可怕了！謝謝你再度救了我！」沈默了一段時間，她又問：「我會死嗎？」

「妳不會有事的。」羅利回答道。

艾美嘆息道：「我還沒交過男朋友。我還沒有嚐過接吻的滋味，我不要死。」

羅利聽了覺得很不捨，便幽默地說：「別擔心！在妳死前我一定會親吻妳的。」

[第八章] 病中受到細心照料的貝絲

p. 60 艾美必須接替喬的兼差工作，伴隨在馬區嬸婆身邊，但是她不知道到底要待多久。她每天為貝絲祈禱，心裡明白自己有多愛和多想念姐姐們。

令人驚訝的是，馬區嬸婆對艾美非常慈祥。小艾美讓這顆老邁的心展現出柔軟的一面。馬區嬸婆盡可能地逗艾美開心。

艾美發現顯然喬對馬區嬸婆有偏見，畢竟她對馬區嬸婆的壞印象都來自於喬的抱怨。

艾美單純地當作是花點時間陪馬區嬸婆，而事情也就沒什麼難的了。兩人都很喜歡有對方為伴。

p. 61 此時，在馬區家，喬和梅格討論著是否應該連絡馬區太太，因為她們完全不知道貝絲的病能不能治癒。

梅格認為，應該讓馬區太太留在父親身邊，但喬卻覺得那樣太被動了。

眼前就連最小的感冒，她都擔心會要了貝絲的命。畢竟貝絲多年來肺部老毛病能好起來，就是靠馬區太太不斷細心照料。

只有馬區太太知道怎麼處理。父親和妹妹兩邊都需要母親的照顧，喬和梅格必須做出選擇。然而在考慮到馬區太太回程的火車票花費後，她們進退兩難的處境似乎更難解決了。

　p. 62　當喬正在照顧貝絲的時候，梅格和羅倫斯先生領著一位中年先生出現了。羅倫斯先生說：「我請我的私人醫生，班醫生，為這個小女孩做個詳盡的檢查。」

　　「喔，救命恩人！」喬興奮地喊。

　　她非常希望醫生能夠救回貝絲，因為她從母親的醫學雜誌上得知，新科技研究帶來許多現代化發明，例如 X 光檢查和藥品，讓醫生能夠有效治療各種疾病。

　　檢查過後，醫生卻表示他無能為力。「很抱歉，現在唯一能做的，只有祈禱奇蹟出現，最好還是通知妳們的母親。」

　p. 64　喬和梅格聽了立刻流下眼淚。此時羅利衝進馬區家並大叫：「我連絡上在華盛頓的約翰了，他會安排馬區太太搭明天一早的火車回來。」

　　月圓時分，窗外的橡樹在嚴寒的風中搖曳，地板上映射出怪異的倒影。喬整夜無眠，一些貓頭鷹的叫聲譜成了旋律，迴盪在她心中，聽來簡直像是一種神奇的咒語，喬心想。她整個人整顆心都傾注在如何擊退貝絲的病。

　　她默禱有超能力能治好妹妹，同時又不斷燒開水更換貝絲貼身的熱水袋，就像記憶中看過馬區太太做的一樣。

　p. 65　馬區太太在破曉時抵達家門。梅格跟著她去看仍在昏睡的貝絲，正好在沙發上小憩的喬也醒來了。馬區太太檢視了一會兒貝絲的病況，便快速地捲起袖子，開始照顧的工作。

她説：「喬，在黃銅臉盆裡裝點醋水，順便拿幾塊乾淨的布巾來。梅格，去拿我的醫藥箱。」沉著的馬區太太接著又吩咐：「我得讓她退燒。妳們一起幫她，增加她的血液循環。」

馬區太太移開貝絲的毛毯之後，開始用熱醋水擦她的四肢，直到熱度降下來。

[第九章] 難以忘懷的聖誕節

■ p. 66 ■ 當陽光從最深的夜空射出，貝絲從沈睡中醒來。最先映入眼簾的是她的母親。高燒耗盡了她的體力。溫暖的臂彎環繞著她，讓她依偎著，她的臉上只是掛著淺淺的微笑。不一會兒她又睡著了。

歸功於馬區太太的照顧，幾個星期以來，貝絲的臉龐再度煥發著神彩光芒。隨著健康情況日漸好轉，她的胃口也好起來了。然而她的身體還是十分僵硬和虛弱。

■ p. 67 ■ 貝絲需要活動活動四肢，於是喬每天半扶半抱地讓她在房子四處走動。先前死亡的恐懼不再盤據著馬區家，已渾然消散了。

聖誕節將近時，馬區家又再度充滿了真正歡愉的氣息。艾美及時從馬區嬸婆家回來，隨母親與姐姐們一同讀馬區先生的信。

當聽到父親打算在新年前回家，女孩們熱烈地歡呼起來。對馬區家人來説，這是多麼幸福並令人振奮啊！越過了重重阻礙，馬區家人盼望已久的全家團圓，終於要來臨了。

■ p. 68 ■ 等到興奮的情緒稍退，喬便帶著貝絲到樓上休息。羅利正好來訪，為馬區家帶來另一個好消息。

「我的祖父希望把一架本來屬於我母親的鋼琴送給貝絲。雖然有點舊，但是製作精良，保存得很好。」羅利説。

「他太慷慨了！對貝絲來説，這是多棒的禮物。她的舊琴琴鍵壞了。喔，她會很喜歡這個禮物的。」喬興奮地説。

「羅利，請向你的祖父轉達我的謝意。明天我想要邀請你們兩位一起吃聖誕大餐。」馬區太太回答道。

「我們用鋼琴給貝絲一個驚喜吧！」艾美玩心大起地提議。

p. 69　到了傍晚，羅利負責把新琴送到馬區家，又把舊琴運走。馬區家的女孩們，除了貝絲正在休息外，都雀躍不已，不動聲色地擦拭著新鋼琴。

她們用馬區太太縫製的一塊美麗衣料將琴蓋住，還在上面用亮紅的緞帶綁了個蝴蝶結當作裝飾。甚至整個房間也運用飾品與蠟燭來點綴。她們想要帶給貝絲一個最難忘的經驗。

第二天當喬背著貝絲下樓，所有的人包括馬區嬸婆、羅利和他的祖父，都圍在鋼琴旁送上驚喜。貝絲心中百感交集。

p. 70　當她解開鋼琴的包裝，淚水就順著臉頰滑下。她太過感動，一時間無法將心中的感激之情都化為言語。她慢慢走向鋼琴，敲了幾個鍵，然後開始彈奏。

她將所有的溫柔情感都化為微妙的音符，娓娓道來。演奏者風姿優雅，琴音充滿磁性，讓聽眾們立刻深深著迷，沈醉其中。馬區家人和歡樂的客人們一齊唱出愉悅的歌聲。他們在屋裡圍成一圈，興高采烈地隨性跳起舞來。

[第十章] 梅格的未來和全家團聚

p. 72 　聖誕節過後，貝絲彈奏的美妙琴音，猶在耳邊清晰地迴盪。由於馬區先生終於要回家了，對馬區家來說，過節的氣氛更加濃厚。

　　午後，馬區太太和梅格在廚房中準備晚餐。梅格告訴母親關於約翰向她求婚的事。

　　馬區太太告訴梅格：「我想妳訂婚後還要等上一段時間。我預計至少三年後才要把妳嫁掉。」

　　喬在走進廚房時無意中聽到這段對話，眼看著將失去她的姐姐，喬感到非常沮喪。

p. 73 　她打斷了她們，質問梅格：「妳說妳要嫁給布魯克先生？他根本是個超乏味的人。」

　　「約翰非常貼心且善解人意。他每天都去醫院探望妳父親。」馬區太太為約翰說話。

　　喬無意中表達了對約翰的反感：「梅格，妳起碼可以嫁個有趣的人吧？就算不有趣，至少是個有錢人。」喬又轉向馬區太太說：「媽媽，不能隨便誰向她求婚，妳就讓她嫁給誰。他太窮了，不能讓梅格過好日子！」

　　梅格終於開口道：「我喜歡布魯克先生。他是個脾氣溫和的好人。他溫柔、親切又認真。而且我不怕窮。」

p. 74 　「錢的確很重要，但是我希望我的女兒們永遠不會因為受錢所迫，而放棄追求生活的真諦，」馬區太太解釋道。

　　「我只希望約翰擁有一個穩固的經濟來源，讓他能夠維持足夠的收入，不至於欠債，讓梅格能安心過日子。女兒們能不能獲得輝煌的財富、時髦的工作或虛名，我都不在乎。如果社會地位和錢財同時伴隨愛與品德而來，我自然樂於接受並充滿感激。」

p. 75 「但是人生經驗告訴我，一間平凡卻能遮風避雨的小屋，就足以承載無數的快樂，確保你不受任何傷害。我很高興看到梅格開始懂得謙卑了。我相信擁有一顆好男人的心，她一定會變得富足，並且成為一個好母親。深掘喜悅之井，汲取靈感之泉，保存生活中幸福的點點滴滴，比獲取錢財更有價值。」

「所以妳不介意約翰很窮？」梅格紅著臉問。

「不會，但是我倒希望他能有一棟房子。」馬區太太回答。

p. 76 「婚姻真是沒有道理！為什麼我們必須結婚？為什麼不能一切照舊？」喬抗拒地說。

「這只是求婚，還沒有決定任何事，」馬區太太說，「現在，女兒們，準備一下！妳們父親隨時都會到。」

傍晚，馬區先生一抵達家門，全家都沈醉在狂喜中。晚餐後，女孩們和她們的母親在客廳裡圍著馬區先生坐下。接下來整個晚上，她們都聽著父親敘述他如何從戰爭中生還的偉大傳奇，也為那些在戰場上失去所愛的人感到遺憾。

這是幾年來頭一遭，馬區家終於能夠完全放鬆下來。當曙光從東方地平線上升起，每個人都感到煥然一新，做好準備迎接嶄新的一天。

[第十一章] 婚禮與求婚遭拒

p. 78 時光飛快地流逝。四年後的某一天，當門廊上的長莖玫瑰清早綻放出光彩，梅格和約翰結婚了。梅格自己就像一朵綻放的玫瑰。「我不想要一個鋪張的婚禮，只要能被所有我愛的人包圍，在他們面前流露真切自我就足夠了。」梅格這樣告訴妹妹們與母親。

於是她縫製了自己的結婚禮服，領子上縫上精細的蕾絲，裙襬周圍則繡上白色滾邊。

p. 79　戶外的布置隆重優雅，完全將梅格和約翰宣誓時刻的神聖光輝襯托出來。為了慶祝馬區家的第一個婚禮，草坪上架起了一座拱門作為紀念，上面綴滿了松針與野花。

所有賓客洋溢著喜悅，三三兩兩分散在花園裡，前去向新娘與新郎道賀。

喬學著讓自己看來從容大方，就算稱不上優雅。她的臉龐神清氣爽，雙眼閃著柔和的光彩。她向來犀利的嘴巴，在今天也變得溫和了。

p. 80　貝絲比過去都要更纖瘦、蒼白和安靜。即使始終沒有完全康復，她也甚少抱怨而總是滿懷希望地說「就快痊癒了」。

艾美被當成「家中的掌上明珠」，因為才十六歲的她，已經展現出女人的萬千儀態了。從她的體型線條，到雙手的舞動，毫不做作而流暢協調，打動了許多人。

馬區夫婦非常以女兒們為傲，堅持只有最好的男人才配娶她們。

p. 81　梅格和約翰的婚禮結束後，喬和羅利到林間小徑中散步。

羅利嘆了口氣，有如山谷間繚繞的一抹薄霧。「為什麼我不能隨心所欲？好比當個作曲家？」

「誰阻撓你了？」喬問。

「我畢業後，祖父要我去歐洲學商，最後做個經濟學家。」羅利回答。

「你不覺得你該決定自己的未來嗎？」喬詫異地說。

p. 82 「我必須順從祖父，不過說真的，我沒辦法想像沒有妳的未來。我覺得我們應該結婚。」羅利跪下來堅定地說。但喬卻搖著頭說：「羅利，我們是摯友，你應該知道我沒興趣當一位妻子。」

「祖父創辦了一間分支遍及世界的貿易公司，我們可以到每個想去的地方旅行，」羅利繼續說，「有一天，我會繼承所有家族財產，妳可以擁有所有妳從未擁有的東西。」

「我配不上你，羅利，」喬鐵了心答道，「我覺得我們沒辦法在一起，因為我們個性太像了，所以總是爭吵。」

「我可以改，我答應永遠不和妳吵架。」羅利搖著喬這樣強調。

p. 84 「我認為真愛應該建立在像我們這樣真誠的友誼上。只要妳接受我的求婚，婚禮可以隨妳的心意無限延期。」

「我很抱歉，羅利，我做不到。」喬最後擠出了這幾個字。

喬的回應就像猛烈的雷雨，瞬間遮蔽了羅利的雙眼。當喬還像塊木頭一樣不為所動，他彷彿像隻受傷的公牛跑開了。日落時分林間閃耀的太陽，射出了死寂的光線。沒人知道羅利和喬的友誼是否就將這樣告終，但是未來一切絕對都會不一樣了。

［第十二章］始料未及的改變

p. 86 艾美嘗試並琢磨各種繪畫形式。她早期的速寫展現出極為生澀的業餘素質。如今她進步許多，作品已贏得數個美術比賽的獎項。

最後艾美決定專攻最精細的鋼筆畫。她擁有鋼筆畫的鑑賞力和技巧，作品中展現的特質可供鑑賞，也具備商業價值。

她為商店與戲院設計海報來賺錢，賺來的錢除了用來支付更多的繪畫消耗品，也用來替自己的畫作裱框，送給家人和朋友。

p. 87 什麼都無法影響艾美的藝術創作。就算顏料不慎濺在畫布上，她還是能畫出有趣的抽象畫。

天氣好的話，她就外出寫生，可以連續坐在潮溼的草地上好幾個小時。

陪伴馬區嬸婆時，她往往大聲朗讀書本。這些書擴展了她的歷史和藝術知識。

梅格的婚禮過後，馬區嬸婆和馬區夫婦談論了艾美的未來。

「我覺得去歐洲藝術學校上課會讓艾美受用無窮。」馬區嬸婆建議。「跟著世界上最頂尖的老師，她可以接受系統性的訓練。而且，她還可以鑽研泥塑、製陶和雕刻方面的技巧。」馬區嬸婆熱切地表達自己的看法。

「但是，那樣花費太高了！」馬區夫婦說。

p. 88 「贊助她我再樂意不過了，畢竟我一向就嚮往到歐洲去，也喜歡有她作伴，」馬區嬸婆繼續說，「更別說現在這裡越來越難找到好對象。但在歐洲可就不同了，她碰到合適對象的機會大多了。」

馬區夫婦對看一眼，都同意馬區嬸婆的話。

傍晚才降臨，當艾美還沉浸在馬區嬸婆慷慨解囊，讓她去歐洲念書的興奮中時，喬面帶愁容地回到家。「怎麼了？」艾美問。

173

當貝絲一抱住喬，喬便崩潰流淚道：「我拒絕了羅利的求婚。」

　p. 90 「我相信妳可以挽回一切的，那只是個誤會，對嗎？」艾美試著安慰喬。

　　「不，我很清楚我真正想要什麼，我無法讓自己變成他的妻子。他一定很恨我，我們就永遠不能再相見了。我只能離開。」喬無助地哭著。

　　「馬區嬸婆要去歐洲。」艾美說。

　　「歐洲！那太理想了！我願意忍受一切去那裡！」喬立刻回答。

　　「但是馬區嬸婆要我陪她去。因為移民法規定她只能帶一個人。嗯，我就是她選上的那個人……」艾美的回答有小小的罪惡感，「但也許她不會介意當我們不在的時候，妳住進她的房子裡。」艾美才說完，喬便覺得更沮喪了。

　p. 91 「當然馬區嬸婆比較喜歡艾美，」當晚喬向母親抱怨，「我又醜，又不善於陪伴她，我總是說錯話。我拒絕了一個理想的求婚，傷了最好的朋友。媽媽，我愛這個家，但是我不能忍受待在這裡了！我一定得做些改變。」

　　「喬，妳有很多不凡的天賦，怎麼可能奢望過一個平凡的人生？」馬區太太帶著鼓勵的微笑說。

　　「儘管我會很想妳，但是妳已經準備好去外面的世界闖蕩，好好揮灑妳的天賦才能。去吧，好好享受自由，看看會有什麼美好的事物等著妳。」

　　一週以後，馬區太太替喬安排一切，讓喬放心離家。這是喬第一次遠離家鄉。

[第十三章] 喬在紐約的新生活

p. 92 馬區太太在紐約的朋友，寇克太太，欣然接受喬成為自己女兒的家教。教書的工作讓喬能夠自立，還能挪出空閒時間寫作賺錢。

喬滿心期待且十分渴望前往紐約，因為舒適的家已經變得像個小小的溫室，對她那喜歡求變的天性來說，有太多限制；對她那顆熱愛冒險的心而言，也過多保護。

p. 93 當喬到達時，寇克太太熱情地迎接她。「親愛的，現在起就把這裡當作自己家。」寇克太太像母親一樣摟著喬說。「為了照顧這間旅舍，我每天從早忙到晚。現在我終於可以放下心來，因為有妳幫我照料孩子們。如果妳想找人聊聊，總是可以在這裡找到一些親切的對象。夜晚妳儘管自由安排。」

她們來到穿堂盡頭的一個房間，寇克太太繼續說：「有什麼事就來找我，我的房門永遠為妳而開，我也會盡力讓妳住得舒適。我為妳準備了一套乾淨床單。現在我要去處理僱用清潔工的事情，以填補之前的空缺。」

她急急忙忙地離開，留下喬在新房間裡自行安頓。喬體會到一種從未有過的隱私感。稍晚，喬寫了封信回家。

p. 94

親愛的媽媽和貝絲：

寇克太太親切地歡迎我，雖然身處在一個滿是陌生人的大房子裡，我還是馬上就有家的感覺。我的房裡有個合用的桌子，緊靠窗邊，光線充足，我可以隨時隨意寫作。大理石地板太涼，所以我把媽媽親手做的地毯鋪上，果然好多了。

我教書的地方是間令人心情愉悅的幼兒房，就在寇克太太的私人客廳旁邊，兩個小女孩非常討人喜歡。剛來到紐約這個大城市，我得承認身處在人叢中，並不輕鬆自在。

　　一般民眾、海軍軍官、水手和各國的移民都帶著他們的行李貨物，從世界各地航行抵達自由女神之都。他們全湧進這座混凝土建構的都市叢林中。這裡和我們康科特的老家毫無共通之處。

p. 96

　　用餐時間，寇克太太旅舍裡的咖啡廳總是人滿為患。聽說他們的豬排配上特製醬汁非常美味，所以我品嚐了，果真名不虛傳，分量很足，是附近最划算的。難怪寇克太太建議我起早去吃，以避開大排長龍的人潮。

　　寇克太太覺得我來到這裡，是為了「屈服於不可避免的婚姻宿命之前，尋求一段滿足感官享樂的人生體驗」。在這樣一個令人眼花撩亂的大城市裡，「吃喝玩樂的體驗」自然是唾手可得，但我希望獲得的體驗，僅僅是文學上的體驗，然後可以盡可能地激發我的寫作。我相信自己的筆遠比刀劍有力，我亟欲成為一名偉大的作家，為人類貢獻自己的力量。

愛你們的
喬

[第十四章] 喬的新朋友

p. 97　一天早晨，當喬吃早餐時，她看到迎面走來一名紳士，幫一位年長的服務生把堆滿髒碗盤的沉重托盤搬到咖啡廳後面的廚房。她記得父親常說：「從小事見真性情。」

　　當晚，她一向寇克太太提起這件事，寇克太太便笑著回答：「那一定是鮑爾先生，他就是這樣的人。」

這天，喬和一位出版商相約會面，努力開展她的事業。她編寫幾個章節的初稿，並製作一份故事大綱。

p. 98 然而，出版商對她的故事並沒有多大興趣。「巫婆、武士、暴怒的野獸？我不想冒犯您，馬區小姐，但是也許您應該試試投稿女性雜誌。我們的讀者不願再花時間沉溺在童話世界中了。」出版商的評語讓喬感到很沮喪，當場就離開了。

在擁擠的大街上遊蕩，喬撞到了一個男人，她的手稿也散落在泥濘的地上。「抱歉！」男人說，露齒而笑，有幾分熟悉。

「我見過你在咖啡廳裡幫忙端東西。」喬一認出是鮑爾先生後便大聲呼叫。

p. 100 「喔，是的，我也記得妳。我們住在同一間旅舍。真是對不起。我想請妳到我那兒喝杯咖啡，讓我把妳的稿子都清乾淨！」鮑爾先生提議，展現出迷人的異國口音和禮貌，喬也就欣然同意了。

「妳知道當我第一次見到妳，我就想……『啊！她是個作家！』」鮑爾先生說。

「是什麼讓你那樣想？」喬問。

他指出她那沾上墨水汙漬的手指就是作家的典型特徵。他接著倒了兩杯咖啡，其中一杯給喬。她啜了一口，但幾乎要吐出來。「妳離鄉背井是嗎，馬區小姐？想家嗎？」鮑爾先生問。

「非常想，特別是我的姐妹們和羅利。」

「她是妳的女性朋友嗎？」鮑爾先生這樣猜。

「不，他是我的男性好友。我們是鄰居。」

p. 101 喬説完後，兩人便突然沈默下來，直到鮑爾先生再度開口問：「咖啡好喝嗎？」

「喔……很濃，但是我很喜歡。」喬微笑著回答。

喬看著周圍讚嘆道：「這裡有好多書！」

「為了辦護照和買船票到這裡，我賣掉了書以外的全部東西。」鮑爾先生答。

「你看來知書達禮，讓我猜猜，你是圖書館館長？化學家？還是心理學家？」喬問。

「在柏林，我是大學的哲學教授兼講師，」他回答，「但在這裡我只是個卑微的代課老師。」

「跟一位哲學家。」喬替他加上這個稱號。

他再度露齒笑著，並遞給喬一本書，「我寫的，在德國出版。」

p. 102 喬很快地看了看那本書，問道：「有沒有英文譯本？」

「也許有一天我們能夠一起合作翻譯。」他説。

喬點頭同意，又好奇地問，「你還要回柏林嗎？」

「大概不，我在那裡沒有家了。」他回答。

那天稍晚，喬寫信回家。

親愛的媽媽和貝絲：

　　我和一位新朋友聊天，度過了一個平靜的夜晚。謝天謝地，我終於在紐約交到朋友了。他非常親切又充滿活力，加上說話機智風趣，帶給我莫大的愉悅。我會持續一週寫一封信，報告這裡的生活。祝妳們有個美好的夜晚，明天更是開心的一天。

愛你們的
喬

[第十五章] 悄悄滋生的愛苗

p. 104

……他窮得就跟我們想像中的哲學家一樣。然而隨著一週一週過去，我卻覺得他比這間旅舍裡的任何人都要慷慨大方……

愛你們的
喬

　　由於寫信回家已成為喬的例行公事，她不得不承認在她的信中，鮑爾先生占據了重要的位置。她必須在信中添加別的事情來掩飾自己，例如看到穿高跟鞋的女人踩著陡峭的樓梯往上爬，以及在離婚率居於全國之冠的紐約市，有越來越多的破碎家庭。

p. 105 儘管喬確切感到她和鮑爾先生之間的吸引力，目前她仍寧願享受單純和他交朋友的感覺。

　　同一時期，在歐洲大陸忙著學習繪畫技巧的艾美，也展開了屬於她的故事。

　　當她漫步在棕櫚樹林立、長滿花朵以及熱帶灌木的花園小徑上，她畫下了最幽靜的景緻。她恣意地捕捉大自然的壯美，不論是穿越濃厚雲層的光束，還是自波平如鏡的湖面上橫渡的鳥群。

　　艾美也發現了鎮上遊行隊伍的迷人之處。一天，她試著畫下一些以羽毛與皮草作成，在狂歡節中用來妝點歡愉氣氛的華麗裝束。

p. 106 人群中，一名年輕人將手背在身後緩慢地走過，看來有點心不在焉。他長得像義大利人，穿得像英國人，但生性則像是不受拘束的美國人。

儘管四周有許多漂亮的臉龐值得眷戀，他卻不屑一顧，直到他的視線落在正專心畫畫的艾美身上。他凝視著她一會兒，接著表情變得雀躍。他急趨到她身旁，拍了拍她的肩。

「喔，羅利，我真不敢相信你也在這裡。我以為你永遠不會來了！」艾美大叫。她站起身擁抱他，任筆刷從膝上掉落。

「我在路上耽擱了，但是我答應要來看妳，所以現在我出現了。」

p. 108 艾美近距離看著他，並暗暗生出一種不曾有過的覷腆。因為羅利變了，她所認識的是過去那個臉龐洋溢著歡樂的男孩，而不是眼前這個滿臉憂鬱的男人。

儘管他比過去更為英俊，但當臉上那抹與老友重逢的歡愉紅暈褪去後，他卻看來疲累而無神。

羅利的到訪從一週延長到一個月。他對於獨自四處遊蕩感到厭倦，艾美這個舊識的出現，似乎為異鄉的風景添了一筆熟悉的風韻。

p. 109 他送給她成堆的禮物，從手製禮服到高級名牌，並且帶她欣賞交響樂和歌劇。然而，真正讓艾美感到煩惱的，是他那滿是浮誇、一點也不謙虛的言談舉止。

她擔心羅利會變成物質的奴隸。可是，她又有點害怕與他爭論會讓他掃興，反而使他變本加厲。

艾美深思著如何正確表達自己的意思，並明白她與羅利之間的感情顯然日益漸深，交織出一種難以解開也無從言喻的複雜情結。

[第十六章] 超越不朽的愛

`p. 110` 春天來臨，當喬回到家，貝絲的改變讓她極為震撼。這些變化是一點一滴累積，不足以讓每天看到她的人吃驚，因此似乎沒有人察覺到。然而，由於喬離家許久，所以一見到妹妹的臉，她馬上就覺得不對勁，心中彷彿壓了一塊大石頭。

貝絲的臉上顯現出一種遙遠而淡漠的表情，彷彿整個人正慢慢從世界剝離；那虛弱的身軀，帶著難以形容而楚楚可憐的美，靈魂本體似乎失去了生命力。喬看見也感受到了，一時間卻什麼也沒說。

`p. 111` 不過第一印象很快地被沖淡，因為貝絲看來很快樂。沒人懷疑貝絲正在逐漸好轉，也沒人警覺到她實際上越變越糟。

喬回到紐約後開始在她的寫作中注入新的風格。她瀏覽桌上成堆的報紙和各種資料標題，鑽研耐人尋味的犯罪新聞，為她的故事架構鋪陳。

在跟出版商約定見面之前，除了新章節的創作外，喬也刪除了過於虛幻不實的元素。出版商的評語是正面的，喬也得到了一紙合約。

她立刻擬妥備忘錄，訂出故事大綱和完成日期。

`p. 112` 幾週後，喬完成了大部分的稿子，並且拿給鮑爾先生看，希望在最後一次修改以前聽聽他的正面建議。

「寫作不只是把動詞、名詞、形容詞和連接詞，合乎語法地擺在一起，」鮑爾先生衝口而出，「我不得不說，為什麼妳不敢寫出真實的想法，照亮內心的黑暗面，而是選擇假裝什麼都不知道？妳必須從妳的成長背景出發，揭開靈魂的最深處，否則妳的書根本毫無價值。」

這真是對喬的自尊充滿羞辱的一擊！她沮喪極了。

p. 113 「這就是我能寫出來的東西，如果它達不到你的高標準，我只能說抱歉。」才說出自己的感受，喬的淚水便滾出了眼眶。她直接回到房間，晚餐時間也沒出現。

約在午夜時分，寇克太太敲了她的房門，送來一封對她打擊更深的不幸電報。上面寫道：「貝絲病重，請速回家。」喬的心凍結了。

她祈求上帝憐憫可憐的妹妹，而天一亮她便啟程回家。

p. 115 「喔，貝絲！在這個世界上我愛妳勝過任何人。妳一定要撐下去！」喬依偎在妹妹身邊這樣說。

「就算是死亡也無法讓我們分離，我不再感到害怕了。」貝絲虛弱地對喬說。「替我照顧爸爸媽媽，如果這樣孤獨一人努力很辛苦，記得我的愛會永遠圍繞在妳身邊。愛是唯一一樣至死也不會消失的東西。有了愛，就可以坦然面對死亡了。」

在追思會上，貝絲看來就像只是睡著了一樣。她離去的哀傷很快就會平復了，因為梅格懷孕了。不只新生命即將降臨馬區家，另一個驚喜也要隨著艾美回來了。

[第十七章] 舊的回憶和新的啟發

p. 116　喬寫了信給艾美，通知她貝絲的死訊。不幸的是，艾美沒有及時收到信而來不及趕回來參加葬禮。而且，馬區嬸婆病得厲害，也禁不起隨艾美跨海跋涉。

　　艾美在回信中明確表示，一旦馬區嬸婆情況好轉，她將儘快安排回程，希望能趕上和家人一同慶祝梅格寶寶的誕生。

p. 117　貝絲的葬禮過後，喬難以將自己從傷心的黑洞中釋放出來。

　　由於是唯一住在家中的女兒，喬一方面要安慰父母，一方面所有時間都被生活瑣事占據。然而，在空閒的時間裡，不論看向何處，舊的記憶總在她心頭纏繞。

　　穿堂沾滿灰塵的架上躺著貝絲的工作靴，貝絲過去常穿的海軍藍圍裙也還掛在廚房的椅背上。失去了摯愛的妹妹，喬受到了太大打擊而無法走出來。她擔心自己此生都將承受這個心靈上的殘缺之痛。

　　「什麼時候我們才能再度在一起？」她憂傷地自問。

　　她還寫了封憂喜參半的信給羅利，告訴他貝絲的死和梅格將為人母的消息。

p. 118　白天裡通常喬是忙碌的，痛苦與寂寞的感覺因而暫時麻痺了。

　　但是當太陽沉入地平線，喬便開始整理舊東西，束之高閣。

　　她發現一個陳舊的寬口箱，想起貝絲常說那是她的藏寶箱。喬的手指緩慢地移到木頭雕刻的把手，卻遲疑著該不該打開它。幾秒鐘後，她振作自己，任由舊的回憶將她帶離現實。

藏寶箱裡有艾美親手做的一副撲克牌、喬過去常玩的弓箭、還有梅格最愛的舊裙子上頭的花布。

p. 120　所有這些早就被姐妹們拋卻的小東西，貝絲卻一直珍藏著。還有一個姐妹們時常用來練習寫字與畫畫的石板，以及一個母親用來記錄每個人的出生日期、眼睛與頭髮顏色和出生時體重的小冊子。

　　看到另一枚父親為了獎勵幼小的貝絲戰勝病魔，而送給她的黃銅勳章，更是讓喬的心擰了一下。

　　喬無法克制地端詳貝絲藏寶箱裡的每樣東西，咀嚼那些東西背後的故事。

[第十八章] 新生命的見證

p. 121　喬的思緒像受無形重力牽動的原子一樣游移，一瞬間，所有記憶的碎片都重新在她心中拼湊出一幅完整的畫面。她挖出手提打字機，開始寫下一個真實的故事。

　　故事中的女主角就是她自己和姐妹們。沒有複雜的情節，喬只是重現那些生命記憶中溫馨的點點滴滴。她懷著無比的樂趣寫著，而最終，她的字字句句都將打動世上所有的婦女。

p. 122　微寒的秋風拂過，在歐洲大陸上某個城市的郊區，羅利帶著行李抵達旅館大廳與艾美會面。

　　過去幾個月來，他幫助祖父處理跨國商務，工作十分辛勞。他成功挽救瀕臨破產的公司，甚至還超越競爭對手。

　　羅利深信這是個向艾美求婚的好時機，但是由於馬區嬸婆臥病生命垂危，他的計畫不得不踩煞車。馬區嬸婆沒有受到太多痛苦，於幾天後過世了。之後很快地，羅利和艾美搭船踏上返家之途。

p. 123 而在美國康科特這一邊，馬區全家緊張地在梅格與約翰家中等待。

「恭喜！」產婆打開臥室房門對約翰道賀，梅格成功產下了寶寶。

「是男孩還是女孩？」約翰趕忙問。

「都是！」產婆費解的回答讓約翰感到困惑。她接著說，「是龍鳳胎！」

約翰立刻放出響亮的笑聲。當他衝進臥室去看妻子與寶寶時，高興得下巴都要掉下來了。

「可愛的小肉團們，歡迎來到馬區家。」喬抱著新生兒呢喃道，「我是喬姨媽，我等不及要跟你一起玩了，讓我們做好朋友吧！我會帶你們探索這個世界。」她接著表示自己樂於替梅格分擔煮飯與洗碗的苦差事，好讓她心無旁鶩地照顧兩個寶寶。

p. 124 就在此時，一輛馬車短暫地停在馬區家門口後，之後抵達了約翰和梅格家。原來是羅利與艾美，他們及時參與這歡慶的時刻。馬區太太打開前門歡迎羅利。他看向屋內並說：「太好了！每個人都在。我要把我的妻子介紹給你們認識。」接著他向旁移了一步。全部的人都大吃一驚，羅利的妻子，那位站在他身後的年輕小姐，竟是艾美。

羅利和艾美先是接受家人的祝福，接著終於見到兩個家族的新成員──由馬區先生命名為黛希和德米。

「好了，艾美和我預測寶寶的性別，誰要是賭輸了就要請另一個人吃點心。現在既然我們兩人都輸了也都贏了，我們應該請所有的人。」

p. 126 羅利接著命令僕人到他最喜愛的麵包店，買了一打鋪滿各種果仁的布丁，又把祖父接過來，一起享受這個格外歡樂的時刻。

艾美問喬是否介意她與羅利結了婚。「我很驚訝，因為我從沒想過你們兩人會在一起，」喬回答，「但是你們為了追求各自的理想，在異鄉飄泊，卻因此重逢，也很令人欣慰。不過，你們要答應我，一定要住得離家近一點。我不能忍受失去另外一個妹妹。」

p. 127 布丁充滿喜悅的甜美滋味，融化在舌尖，讓每個人滿足而感恩。這個幸福的結尾，對喬筆下那個描述平凡人生活的故事而言，深具代表性。他們一家人已經很久沒有這樣沉醉在團聚的狂喜中了。新生的嬰兒承接逝去的死者，共同替生命灌注了能量，讓喬深受感動，從中獲得全然的力量。

[第十九章] 舊房子新計畫

p. 128 對喬而言，寫作過程就像是獨居在洞穴中。而唯有如此才能讓她無後顧之憂，在文字中發掘真實的自己。相對來說，有人認為那和關在牢裡沒什麼兩樣，差別只在作家是出於自由意志，創造出所謂的人類遺產。

喬駕馭文字的能力漸漸成熟了，她能捕捉不假修飾的情感，她深信那是任何藝術表達的關鍵。

每當靈感湧現，在融入主要故事之前，她會將它先在紙上記錄下來。所有瑣碎細小的線索提示，都在喬這個彷彿訓練有素、觀察細微的間諜手中，優美地編織成冊。

p. 129 最後，到了要將手稿裝進信封寄出時，喬會把故事從頭到尾檢查一遍，確認內容連貫流暢，才在封蠟上留下精細簽名，並寄到紐約聽取鮑爾先生的意見。

馬區嬤婆沒有孩子，但是意外地，她的遺囑卻表明希望喬
繼承她的宅第。

一天，馬區太太和喬前去查看，發現這棟房子除了地點方
便之外，還擁有馬廄、穀倉，以及可就近在湖上遊覽或是釣魚
的船塢。至於房子裡面，從地板、窗戶到家具則都蒙上了一層
灰。

「我從沒注意這裡有這麼多壁爐！不知道煙囪是不是都堵
住了？」喬詫異地說。

「妳需要一個手巧的人來處理修繕問題，還要一名園丁來
種幾棵樹。」馬區太太建議。

p. 130 「真大！這麼大的地方我一個人怎麼
住？」喬問。

「在這個地方開課最適合了，」馬區太
太說出她的看法。

喬十分贊同這個提議，並且興奮地和母
親商量。身為執行主辦者的喬需要得到市長和
教育部門的特別認可，才能實際開課給市民。

既然馬區家早已長期從事社區服務，喬便希望增設課程，
幫助貧苦兒童接受較好的教育。

她的學校自然是屬於非營利機構，也有權接受捐獻，還能
從其中款項扣除稅金。

p. 132 不過，喬還需要更多錢來讓學校運作。她想要邀請職業
演出者在體育館表演募款。馬區太太則從舊識和地方教會的修
女中招募人手，管理志工團隊。

由於近日觀光發展迅速，馬區太太十分看好這個計畫，認
為必定能夠吸引大量人潮，作為長期的經費來源。

經過一番建設性十足的討論，喬回到家，發現有人送來一
份包裹後就離開了。

187

她很快地拆開包裹，發現裡面是她的故事，另外還夾著出版商的一封信與合約。喬自問誰會專程送來這個包裹，想來想去，只有一個可能：鮑爾先生。

[第二十章]愛的歸宿

`p. 134` 　喬迫切地要找出答案，問道：「漢娜！妳知道是誰把包裹送來的嗎？」

　　「半個小時之前，一個中年男人把包裹送來，他的姓很奇怪，說話還帶著外國口音。我猜他是艾美或羅利的朋友，歐洲的外交官之類，是來送結婚禮物的，所以我告訴他馬區小姐嫁給羅倫斯先生以後，就搬到隔壁去了。他聽了便說他得去趕火車而離開了。」

`p. 135` 　「喔，不會吧！」喬大叫著，拔腿匆忙跑向火車站。
　　她的心懸著跳得厲害，腦子則一片空白。
　　當她踏進火車站時，四周人滿為患。她的眼光掃過每張臉，卻都不是她要找的。終於，一個正在幫助身前一名老婦人上車的男人引起了她的注意。「鮑爾先生！」喬全力叫著。
　　他看看四周尋找聲音的來源，但是其他擠著上車的旅客掩蓋了她的聲音。喬站上長凳並繼續大聲呼喚，直到鮑爾先生看到了她。

`p. 136` 　穿過人潮以後，他們終於來到彼此身旁。
　　「讀妳的書就像是一扇窗，可以直視妳的心。我既驕傲又高興，看到妳像花朵一樣美麗地盛開，接納真實的自己。」鮑爾先生讚美道。

「你這麼快就得趕回紐約嗎？」喬問。

「事實上我剛決定搬到西岸。我聽説那邊有很多更多教授職缺。我的朋友説我可以隨時開始替中級德語班代課。」鮑爾先生不太情願地表示。

p. 137 喬告訴鮑爾先生她創設學校的計畫，並問他：「你願意考慮跟我一起工作嗎？我想你是校長的最佳人選。」

在一陣帶著疑惑的沉默後，他尷尬地説：「謝謝妳的邀請，但是我不想打擾妳的婚姻。」

喬立刻澄清道：「喔，不！嫁給羅利的是我妹妹艾美。」

p. 138 對這麼一個具喜劇效果的誤會，他們大笑了好一陣子。之後喬繼續説：「我希望你跟我一起留在這裡，作為我事業和人生的守護者。」喬一番真誠的話語立刻讓鮑爾先生臉上充滿喜悦，彷彿置身天堂一樣。

故事接近尾聲，馬區家也得到了驚人的收穫。根據區所學生與家長的意見調查顯示，由喬和鮑爾先生創立的學校，被評為最優良的私立學校。

喬的小説出版了，並且在全國大賣。她成為當代最具影響力的女性作家。經歷了種種苦難，馬區家終於嚐到豐收的果實，隨著美夢成真，她們會繼續將傳奇人生傳承下去。

Answers

Exercise

P. 140　A.　① d　② c　③ a　④ c　⑤ c
　　　　　　⑥ b　⑦ d　⑧ b　⑨ b　⑩ d
　　　　　　⑪ a　⑫ d　⑬ b　⑭ b　⑮ b
　　　　　　⑯ d　⑰ b　⑱ d　⑲ b　⑳ c

P. 146　B.　(1)
　　　　　　① admiration　　② rage
　　　　　　③ invention　　④ assembled
　　　　　　⑤ satisfy　　　⑥ offended
　　　　　　⑦ inspirations　⑧ inheritance
　　　　　　⑨ mentions　　⑩ assumed

　　　　　　(2)
　　　　　　① necessity　　② economic
　　　　　　③ regularly　　④ comedy
　　　　　　⑤ element　　　⑥ solution
　　　　　　⑦ scarce　　　⑧ invention
　　　　　　⑨ neglected　　⑩ remains

小婦人 【二版】
Little Women

作者 _ 露意莎・梅・奧爾柯特
　　　（Louisa May Alcott）
改寫 _ Winnie Huang
審訂 _ Dennis Le Boeuf / Liming Jing
插圖 _ Nan Jun
翻譯 _ 孫淑儀
編輯 _ 賴祖兒 / 鄭家文
作者 / 故事簡介翻譯 _ 王采翎
校對 _ 陳慧莉
封面設計 _ 林書玉
排版 _ 葳豐 / 林書玉
製程管理 _ 洪巧玲
發行人 _ 周均亮
出版者 _ 寂天文化事業股份有限公司
電話 _ +886-2-2365-9739
傳真 _ +886-2-2365-9835
網址 _ www.icosmos.com.tw
讀者服務 _ onlineservice@icosmos.com.tw
出版日期 _ 2020年10月 二版一刷（250201）
郵撥帳號 _ 1998620-0 寂天文化事業股份有限公司

Let's Enjoy Masterpieces! **Little Women**

國家圖書館出版品預行編目資料

小婦人 / Louisa May Alcott 原著；Winnie
Huang 改寫；-- 二版 . -- [臺北市]：寂天文化，
2020.10
　　　面； 公分 . -- (Grade 5 經典文學讀本)
　　譯自 : Little Women
　　ISBN 978-986-318-938-1(25K 平裝附光碟片)

1. 英語　　2. 讀本

805.18　　　　　　　　　　　　　109012896